THE TWILIGHT OF THE MAGICAL SIREN:
A TALE OF LATE ANTIQUITY

by

Barak A. Bassman

TELEMACHUS PRESS

THE TWILIGHT OF THE MAGICAL SIREN: A TALE OF LATE ANTIQUITY

Cover designed by Telemachus Press, LLC

Cover art:
Copyright © iStock/510324004_kateja_f

Published by Telemachus Press, LLC
http://www.telemachuspress.com

ISBN: 978-1-945330-70-4 (eBook)
ISBN: 978-1-945330-71-1 (paperback)
ISBN: 978-1-945330-72-8 (hardback)

Library of Congress Location Number: 2017949805

Telemachus Press, LLC
7652 Sawmill Road, Suite 304
Dublin OH 43016

10 9 8 7 6 5 4 3 2 1

FICTION / Folklore

Version 2017.07.27

The Twilight of the Magical Siren:
A Tale of Late Antiquity

I. The Mermaid in the Storm

NOT FAR FROM the sleepy port town, in the waning decades of the Roman Empire in the West, was a modest island off the shore upon which sat a lighthouse. On this particular eve Judah, the youthful nighttime lighthouse keeper, sat in the old stone tower peacefully watching a storm unfolding over the waves. Yet, in the lightning flash, he saw something unexpected: a woman jumping out of the sea, arms spread wide, apparently in ecstatic joy amidst the tempest. She had pale skin and thick blue hair, in which he thought he saw red coral garlands. And she had no fear of the surging waves and the booming thunder.

Judah's first thought was to help her, which was, after all, part of his duties keeping watch over the outer harbor. But a terrible fear gripped him. What if he were to die out there? He had not chosen to swim in a thunderstorm. Why should he perish, a young bachelor with so much life still to live, because a suicidal madwoman wanted to bathe in lightning? So Judah concluded it was best to resist the urge to rescue the seemingly unhinged maiden.

The lightning returned in a harsh flash. Something leaped high out of the water–it was her, the same woman, he was sure of it–that same long blue hair. But this time she had hoisted her entire body out of the water. When Judah looked below her waist, there were neither legs nor feet, but instead an immense fish tail swishing rapidly back and forth in the air. There was something else different this time: Judah thought he saw her looking straight at him.

Then the fish-woman descended back into the water, and the lightning faded. Judah quickly downed a cup of strong wine to fortify his spirits. You are seeing things that are not there, he told himself, because you have spent too much time alone in this tower at night. You are losing your reason.

There was another flash, and there she was again, now sitting calmly in the water, with her human head and naked torso visible and her fish tail below. When she saw Judah again staring at her, she smiled back kindly, and ran her fingers through her hair playfully, even flirtatiously. She disappeared again when the lightning faded. Sad he could no longer see her, Judah cursed the cruelty of the old gods of the sea for making sport of him.

But not too much later, as the storm was fading away, a sound wafted up from the sea into the tower–a song, filled with melancholy. The language sounded strange to Judah. It was not the Latin he spoke every day. It sounded Greek, but not the profanity-laden Greek he heard from the sailors from the Empire's Eastern provinces.

Even though he could not understand the words well, the song moved Judah. Its melody spoke of the bittersweet pleasures of solitude. Feeling the singer was serenading him alone because she had seen into his lonely soul, and wished to comfort him, he closed his eyes, inhaled the cool storm night air, and listened.

When Judah opened his eyes again the fish-woman was close enough that he could see her in the light of the stone tower's reflecting mirror. She was singing the seductive Greek dirge. Her body was a dazzling array of color: her hair and eyes were sea blue, her lips and coral crown and necklace were a bright red, and the small part of her fish tail sticking out of the water was a lush green.

She stared at Judah and smiled.

Descending from the lighthouse tower to the narrow, rocky beach below, he saw her close by in the water. There were no ships about in the still night, and, with the storm gone by now, all was silent except for her sad song.

Judah unmoored a wooden boat from the island's dock and rowed out to her as fast as he could. The song now surrounded him, making his whole body vibrate with its rhythm. She soon was swimming right at the edge of the rowboat, her eyes level with his. The fish-woman began stroking Judah's cheek. Up close, he could see hers was an aging, worn beauty, with faintly wrinkled skin and sagging flesh. He wanted only to stay like this, just so, in a special place outside of normal time and everyday worries.

Then she stopped singing, grabbed his cheeks, and kissed him passionately upon his lips before pushing him away and swimming off. He had an impulse to dive after her—but stopped himself, recalling too well the story from the *Odyssey* he had been taught as a little boy, of the sirens who lured sailors to their doom.

Back in the lighthouse tower, Judah looked out on the drab, endless sea and felt many things at once: sadness, loneliness, longing, but also deep joy and love. During this reverie, the pink sliver at the far eastern edge of the horizon gradually spread out and banished the night. It would soon be time for him to leave the isle and its lighthouse, and return to his bed in his parents' stuffy, cluttered home in the solid ground of the city on the mainland.

II. The Priest's Tale

JUDAH SPENT THE next several days dreaming of his magical night. He had trouble paying attention to what anyone said, often losing the thread of conversations or forgetting what he was supposed to do. Everywhere were angry, impatient faces–his mother repeating again she needed him to buy flour, the merchant at the flour stall fuming he had other customers and could not spend his day waiting for Judah to wake up and pay him, the other customers in the marketplace always bumping into Judah and shouting at him to pay attention and get out of people's way.

The nights in the lighthouse brought no relief. Judah longed to see the siren again, but she was nowhere to be found. At every splash or ripple in the sea, no matter how insignificant, he would eagerly rush down to the beach at the foot of the tower, but to no avail: the sea calmed and he gave up, plodding heavily back up the steps of the tower, with sighs of self-pity.

One night, a ship entered the area illuminated by the lighthouse, in front of which he saw a giant woman swimming. She had a long fish tail, but her hair was pink instead of blue, and her skin had a deathly yellow pallor. Still, Judah was not in a mood to quibble over such details. His siren had come back, he would kiss her again, and–and he did not know what else, uncertain what one did with a beautiful siren other than, like the sailors' old legends, jump to your death.

The siren loomed larger as the ship approached, although oddly frozen in her gestures. Racing down onto the beach, Judah mounted a boulder to spy his beloved, but as she at last drew near his heart sank: she was a wooden sculpture, tacked onto the ship's prow and painted garishly–a fake wooden siren, another snide trick of the shadows of the sea at night. Judah slumped down on the rock, picking at the lichen as he watched the mock siren bob up and down in the waves until she docked in the port.

One week passed this way, and then another, and then a third. He no longer spoke with his parents or his brothers. They would slap him on the back, drain a cup of wine, and regale him with stories of business successes or their hackneyed opinions on the importance of taking a wife and begetting children for a fine young Jewish man. Judah would notice their loud sounds and hot breaths and nod along. Eventually the noise of these voices grew too bothersome, interfering with his attempts to relive in his memory the kiss with the siren. Sometimes, in the middle of one of these bombarding monologues, Judah would simply walk away in the direction of the shore. He now understood all too well the urge to jump into the sea after hearing the siren's song.

He eventually resolved to seek counsel from Tobias, the chief lighthouse keeper, an old man with a short and perfectly hairless body, from his totally bald skull down to his legs. Tobias had been the lighthouse keeper for many years now, and lived alone in a small cabin on the islet where the tower stood. This cabin housed precious few possessions: a collection of old scrolls, miniature faded statues of old pagan gods, and a threadbare pantry. With his eyesight and strength failing, he had hired Judah to handle the nighttime shifts, which required more youthful vigor than he had been able to muster anymore.

Tobias had become the lighthouse keeper late in life. For many generations his family had held the priesthood of the nearby port city's temple and shrine to Venus. His ancestors had secured the honor of this hereditary priesthood through their abundant wealth and vast landholdings, pledging to pay for the temple's upkeep and occasional beautification. But, over time, the family fortune had withered away: one relative backed the wrong usurper for the imperial purple, leading the legitimate emperor to confiscate his lands for redistribution to the patriotic soldiers who had vanquished the loathsome rebel; another made a foolish investment in a mercantile voyage to the East that sank to the ocean floor in a faraway shipwreck; and a third gambled away several farming estates. Tobias's family was finally reduced to a shabby gentility, becoming wards of the city's local senate, which now paid them for their priestly services to Venus.

Tobias's father had passed away when he was a young man, forcing his recall from student life in Athens to assume the local priesthood of Venus. He was filled with passion for his goddess. Ever since Constantine the Great's embrace of Christianity, his father and grandfather had watched their flock dwindle while the nearby Christian churches swelled with converts to the new imperial faith. Tobias was determined to show the city's inhabitants that Venus was truly their goddess and protector.

Several years after Tobias assumed the priesthood, Julian the Apostate became Emperor and declared himself openly for the old pagan gods. Many feared there would be a new wave of persecution of Christians, or at least that they were out of favor, so once again prudent, worldly citizens filled the temple of Venus and offered prayers and sacrifices to the old goddess.

Confident the gods had finally turned the tide of history, Tobias demanded the Christian bishop give prayers and sacrificial offerings to Venus. The bishop, a pious and strict Christian, refused. Tobias then marched with a small mob to the bishop's villa, and repeated his demand. Venus's raucous partisans came with torches and clubs, and stank of the wine her young priest had freely distributed to them. He whipped the mob into a righteous frenzy: we must appease the goddess; it is she who protects the city, this blasphemer will infuriate her, and she will wreak destruction upon us all in retribution for his stiff-necked disdain.

Confronted with this mob, the bishop walked out upon his veranda in the full regalia of his office. A tall, slender man, with an aristocratic bearing, he stared down the frenzied crowd and its ranting boy-priest ringleader in calm, mute disgust until at last they became silent.

Then the bishop addressed the crowd: You are all sinners whose punishment will be just and deserved in the next world, if not in this one. If any man wishes to repent and seek salvation from our one true Savior, I shall receive him tomorrow at church.

And with that, the bishop went back inside his villa.

Men at the edges of the crowd began to disperse, and even those in the forefront averted their eyes from each other. Feeling his moment slipping away Tobias rallied again. How dare he! The filthy old man lives under the protection of the good goddess and spits in her face. Burn his house down! Do it now, and the goddess will bless you forevermore!

Tobias tossed a torch through the bishop's window. This bold act inspired others, and the villa was soon in flames. The bishop himself escaped through the back. The province's governor, who had remained a pious Christian, took custody of the bishop to ensure his safety.

Tobias's triumph was short-lived. The Emperor Julian the Apostate died in his Persian campaign less than two years after seizing the throne, thus returning the Christians to power. Now freed from his protective custody, the bishop concluded he had been too tolerant of idolatry, and that the plague of heresy needed to be stamped out before Tobias had another opportunity to molest the faithful of the church.

This time the bishop led his emboldened flock to the steps of Tobias's beloved temple of Venus. This new mob was filled with many former pagan devotees eager to show the genuineness of their return to the true faith. The bishop mounted the steps of the temple, in his full regalia, and approached Tobias standing in the late afternoon shadow of a marble statue of Venus. The bishop towered over the much shorter priest.

Tobias was determined to hold his ground, but he could not stop his body from trembling. There were snickers from the crowd below. The bishop stood silently, gloating as Tobias visibly tried and failed to stop shaking. A puddle of urine formed at Tobias's feet. The snickers grew louder, and the bishop grinned.

The bishop raised his hand to silence his obedient flock and then asked Tobias if he was ready to accept the true faith and to repent of his sins. Tobias squeaked out a weak, faltering no. So be it, said the bishop.

Two burly men grabbed Tobias's arms and pulled him aside. On the bishop's orders Tobias was not harmed—he had to be allowed an opportunity to repent in this life before facing judgment in the next one. The bishop's followers then ransacked the temple. The looted statues and temple treasury were to be used or sold for the church's greater glory.

The hollowed out temple was set on fire and by the next morning was in ruins. The city government later sold the plot of land to a wealthy Christian grain merchant, who built a warehouse there. The goddess was forgotten, as she no longer had a dwelling place in the modest port city.

Without a temple where he could officiate, Tobias was adrift. He had devoted all of his patrimony, meager as it was, to Venus, and that wealth, along with much else, had now been appropriated by his holiness the bishop. Tobias begged for money in the thoroughfares, and what he scrounged up he drank away in the filthiest taverns frequented by the roughest, poorest ship hands. He would sleep in the alleyways, his torn clothes sprinkled with tracks of his own vomit.

At first, the bishop and the friendly Christian authorities took this as a salutary example for the community of the proper fate for arrogant sinners who would persecute pious Christians. Yet, over time, people began to pity Tobias. Memories of his crimes faded, and some leading citizens recalled the many services rendered by Tobias's family to the city. Soon it was generally agreed that Tobias's miserable lot was a scandal, and something needed to be done.

Fortunately for the city's conscience, the incumbent lighthouse keeper chose to move away to a newly inherited estate in a distant province. Tobias was quickly installed in his place. Now everyone could feel fine about themselves: Tobias was gainfully employed and well provided for, but safely exiled to his small island.

Judah's family watched these events unfold with wry detachment. As members of the city's tightly knit, albeit somewhat laxly observant, Jewish community, they did not care much about disputes between rival camps of gentiles, although the violence was worrisome—one never could be sure that the drunken mobs would not turn on the Jews, who had all too conspicuously rejected both the old pagan idols and the new Christian scriptures. In the end, the Jewish community was relieved once the civic peace had been restored.

Judah first met Tobias one afternoon when he was supposed to row out to a ship near the harbor with a message from his father for the captain, but was caught in a storm and washed up on the island where the lighthouse tower sat. Tobias, by now an old man, threw a warm blanket over Judah and helped to repair his boat. While Tobias did not speak about his past, Judah felt there was something magical and otherworldly about him: the old lighthouse keeper had no apparent interest in money or luxuries, his conversation was perfunctory, and there was something distant about his gaze, as if his soul had wandered far away, to somewhere hidden and sacred.

Tobias and the lighthouse soon became Judah's preferred refuge when he could no longer tolerate his parents' discussions of business or why he needed to consider this or that possible marriage match. On the narrow rocky beach, the two men would share warm spiced wine, or sometimes cheese and bread, although they did not speak much to each other, preferring to gaze out silently at the broad horizon. Judah would feel his worries dissolve into the vast eternal sea.

When Tobias confided he could no longer manage his nighttime duties and asked if the young man could perhaps help him from time to time, Judah immediately agreed. Nevertheless, even though they were now colleagues in the lighthouse administration, their conversation remained sparse. Judah dared not question Tobias about his painful past, and Tobias showed little (if any) interest in anyone else's presence.

But now that he was mad with longing for the mysterious siren, Judah had made up his mind to speak at length to Tobias. He had to know if the old lighthouse keeper had ever seen this wondrous sea creature, or could tell him anything about her–maybe even where to find her or how to summon her. After all, he reflected, who else had spent as many lonely nights on that isle straddling the border between the land and the sea, looking out at the water for ships, gods, and monsters?

So one afternoon Judah went early to the lighthouse and found Tobias alone in his cabin, reclining in a wooden chair too big for his frail, bony body, reading a scroll, written in Greek, although Judah could not make out what it said. Tobias paid no attention to Judah. After a few moments of silence, Judah loudly tapped his foot.

Tobias continued to ignore him.

Judah finally spoke up: Brother, friend, I need a word with you, this is an urgent, urgent matter.

Tobias looked up. What's that, eh? Something broken in the old tower?

No, no, the tower is fine. But I must speak to you about her. The siren, the woman with the green fish tail and the blue hair, I saw her and I kissed her, but now she is gone. Am I mad? Have you seen her, in all these years you have spent here, have you seen her?

Tobias put his scroll on the floor and his eyes suddenly focused intensely upon Judah. When did you see her? What did she say? Tell me, tell me everything.

It was a few weeks ago, during the bad storm. She jumped up and down in the waves and when the storm calmed, I rowed out to her. She kissed me. And she sang to me. But she said nothing. That was it, yet I cannot stop longing for her to come back, and she is nowhere to be found. I cannot do anything these days but wander about moaning for her return, I cannot think about anything else, I barely sleep and, even then, I dream only of her. You have seen her, haven't you? How can I find her again?

Tobias smiled sadly and replied: You do not find her, she finds you. You have been blessed and chosen. Who would have imagined she would pick a Jew? You people have been so cruel and unloving to her through the ages, smashing her beautiful statues and refusing her every honor. Well, I suppose you have been good to me, unlike so many others. Maybe that has made you worthy. But this is a great blessing for you, lucky Jew.

Judah sat down on a stool. Who is she? What is she? Is she a siren, who will lure me to my death, to drown myself?

No, Tobias said calmly, she is neither siren nor witch nor monster. She is a goddess. The most beautiful, wondrous goddess. You will see her again, I am sure of it. I first saw her as a little boy. My father was her priest, in her old temple. It was late one night, and I was helping my father clean the altar and the shrines. Back then, people would come and make sacrifices and offerings to her. All those crowds and burnt animal parts and spilled grain offerings created a mess. My father, as the priest, would clean it up. As his only son, I would help.

I must have been five or six years old. My father was exhausted from tending to all her pilgrims and, though he tried his best to finish his labors, he collapsed asleep on a bench. I was the only other one there and I walked up to her statue. I had never been allowed to approach her this closely. I knew I was being bad, but I could not help myself.

She towered over me. There was a skylight in the temple, and at this late hour the bright moon rained its light down upon the goddess's statue. I looked up at her. She was so beautiful, all perfectly sculpted, shining white marble. I felt puny. I wanted her to embrace me, to shelter me, but she was cold and immobile.

That is, she was that way at first. As I stared at her, colors began to emerge from inside the statue, grow brighter, thicker, and become visible—blue hair, red lips, green dress. Life came into those eyes. She bent down and picked me up, and then she stroked my cheek and kissed my forehead. She put me down on the bench by my father, and, as I fell asleep, she sang a song to me, a sweet, melancholy song, but I cannot recall it anymore.

She did not show herself to me again for several years, although I yearned for her and prayed fervently each night for her to hold me in her arms. My mother seemed to be cursed in those days: after me, every child was miscarried or stillborn. Eventually she could not bear the pain of losing so many children. She avoided my father's touch, no doubt to make sure there would never be another pregnancy. She sometimes smothered me with kisses and caresses, but then she would strike me hard on my face and reproach me with terrible, raging curses. I think she was afraid the gods would take me away too, to complete whatever divine vengeance was her lot.

In time, she locked herself in a cramped attic room, crying at first, but later she just stared at the wall, almost lifeless. After catching a chill one bitter winter evening, she drifted away and became a shade in the underworld. I was twelve years old when my mother died.

As I was losing my mother to madness and despair, I longed with ever greater intensity for the goddess Venus to return to me, to cradle me in her perfect everlasting love. I remembered how safe and warm I had felt in her arms, how warm and loving her touch was. I loved her all the more because she did not show herself to me. I suppose an unrequited love, from a distance, is a seductively selfish pleasure.

I took every opportunity to assist my father in her temple, so I could be in her dwelling place and in the shadow of her marble statue: I cleaned animal grease and blood from sacrifices, I washed the blistered and calloused feet of pilgrims who had trudged to our shrine from the countryside, often tramping for days in shoes with barely any sole left on them.

Except for my kind father, everyone kept their distance from me. I made my classmates and teachers uneasy with the way I would tremble all over and water around the eyes when I spoke of my goddess. Even my father tried, ever so gently, to calm me down, explaining that the goddess celebrated love and joy, and that she hoped her followers would find moments of happiness in the world around them. But I did not care. The world and its shallow joys were nothing to me. She was everything.

She returned to me when I was fourteen years old. It was late at night in her temple. My father had gone home, but I insisted on remaining and cleaning. I was dusting her statue, as I recall, when my cheek fell into her marble hand. It was strangely warm, and that warmth made me drowsy. I lay down at her marble feet and drifted to sleep.

In my dream, I was in her temple, but in place of her statue was a large, grey stone throne. There she sat, erect, regal. Her hair was blue, her lips were red, and her dress was green. I was kneeling down in front of her. She stood, bent down, and raised me up by the chin. I was naked and shivering. She took my head in her hands and made me look into her sea blue eyes.

And then she kissed my lips. That kiss was like nothing else I had ever felt—I was filled with light, with joy, and the world spun around at dizzying speed. I cannot recall how long that kiss lasted, but it was the greatest joy I have ever known.

When she pulled away, I pledged my eternal love and devotion to her alone.

Good, she said, stay true to your vow and I shall always protect you.

I awoke with a start. My father was standing over me in the sunlit morning, but he was terrified at what he beheld. I ran to the water basin by the temple doors, where the pilgrims cleaned themselves, to look at my reflection in the water—and saw that all the hair on my body had disappeared. I have been hairless, top to bottom, ever since, even though I have never shaved any of it. Perhaps that was the offering she wanted from me. Or, it was her brand on my body.

A couple of years later I was sent to Athens to complete my studies. It was a wonderful place then, full of philosophy and poetry and men devoted to the true, old gods, not to the Christian god. I made friends, good, dear friends, for the first and last time in my life. We argued metaphysics, declaimed Homer and Theocritus, and drank too much at the taverns.

But in all this headiness I forgot I belonged only to the great goddess. My teacher of rhetoric had a daughter, petite and olive skinned and oval faced, and I fell in love with her. I would stare at her when she would come in and out of the lecture room with food and drink for her father and his students. She was embarrassed, I could see that, but I could not help myself. I made up an excuse to visit the teacher one afternoon. Once I was inside his home, I cornered his daughter, fell to my knees, and declared my love. She recoiled in horror. I can still summon, in my mind, those eyes brimming with disgust. She ran away, and it was made clear to me that I was not welcome back.

I cursed my small, bony, hairless body. I thought I looked like a rodent who had learned to walk upright and speak human language. Of course she despised me, I was ugly and deformed and had no great fortune. Why would she desire me?

Plenty of broad-shouldered, bearded, wealthy boys for her to choose from.

I walked restlessly that night through the streets of Athens, away from the student areas, into the places where the native Greeks take their pleasures, until I found a tavern with peeling walls and dirt-caked floors, where I drank so much cheap wine that I was not sure I could stand up again. The tavern-keeper, a friendly giant with a deep voice, offered a bed in the back for a modest price, where I could sleep it off.

He also pointed to a woman leaning over a table diagonally opposite me. She too was short and olive-skinned, like my beloved, but also fat, middle-aged, and had a jagged, meandering scar on her cheek. I could have her too, he said, for another nominal fee.

In my stupor I paid for both the bed and the woman. After helping me to undress, the tavern-keeper lay me down on the straw bed. He really was a kind man, in his way. After he left the woman entered. Without any fuss or conversation, she undressed and lay down next to me. I did not move. I had no idea what to do.

There she was, on her back, next to me, our thighs touching, waiting for me to do something. I both wanted her to stay and wanted her to leave; it was all a muddle. Is everything okay, sir? she asked. Should I go?

But still I did nothing. So we lay there together, motionless, listening to the loud din from the tavern. Although my heart beat violently, she loudly sighed with boredom.

I suppose she eventually decided to get on with it so she could leave me and move on to more interesting customers. She rolled on top of me, and did what she assumed I wanted her to do. She did not kiss me, though. I did not move, but shut my eyes in shame. When it was done she dressed quickly and left.

I slept a long, black dreamless sleep. The next day I vomited in the street, my head pounded horribly, I itched everywhere—something had bitten me all over in that bed—I was an even uglier rodent than before, a bald rat speckled with little red sores.

Once I had my bearings again, I went straight to the goddess's shrine in Athens, a small establishment (Minerva obviously being the preferred goddess there). I trembled before the statue of Venus and begged her for guidance. A strong wind then came from nowhere, which knocked a clay jar hard against the side of my head. I understood: I had betrayed Venus, and broken my vow to be hers alone. I sobbed and begged her for forgiveness.

After that, I avoided women, but my passions latched onto something far worse: politics, conspiracy and politics. There were excited whispers all over Athens—Julian, the imperial prince, had come to study philosophy, and he was rumored to be a secret adherent of the old, true gods, and to have rejected his family's, the Emperor's, Christianity. There was a frenzy of speculation and plotting. In truth, I did hardly more than make fevered speeches in cramped private rooms with other half-grown boys making their own fevered speeches. But I swore to myself that I would vanquish my goddess's enemies if our party were ever to seize power.

I was summoned home when my father died to assume the priesthood of Venus. I was meticulous in my devotions to her and her temple. As the city was firmly in Christian hands, I said nothing about politics. I also continued to avoid all women, not that anyone was eager to marry me–my hideous rodent body, and my meager income, combined to render me a truly unsuitable husband.

Sometime soon after, my greatest hopes were realized: Julian became emperor and publicly cast off his adherence to Christianity. Now was my opportunity. I began to persecute the Christians in the city. I whipped up mobs with fiery rhetoric. I even burned the bishop's house down. All of this to make amends to the goddess, to stamp out her enemies and prove the sincerity of my devotion.

She did not want me to do this, although I was then too blinded by my vicious passions to see her true wisdom. Once again I was forced to suffer because of my sins. Julian fell in battle, the Christians returned to power, the temple of Venus was looted, and I became a starving, filthy beggar in the streets.

I recalled again the sweet warmth of the kiss of the goddess. I prayed to Venus to appear to me again, to guide and comfort me, and she answered my prayers. It was a perfect spring night, warm, but not oppressively so, without clouds or moon, just a wondrous blanket of glittering stars. I felt a sudden urge to walk to the seashore. Plodding clumsily in my soiled rags, I was a sorry sight, but I made it to the sea all the same. With the last of my strength I stood there, under the stars, quivering with anticipation.

It must have been quite late, as no one else was about, and I heard no sounds but the waves crashing against the rocks. Then I saw her: leaping out of the water was a woman with blue hair and red lips, and a green fish tail. She wore a red coral necklace now, and a red coral crown. She swam to the shore, to me, and stroked my cheek. I trembled with joy and sobbed like a baby. She sang me a sweet lullaby until I calmed down.

She spoke to me: I was born from the sea, from its foam and waves, and I have returned to the sea. Men no longer wish to devote themselves to me; they do not want my help anymore. You promised yourself to me. Join me by the sea. We can be together.

The next morning, I was awoken by the local authorities. They offered me the position of lighthouse keeper. I knew this was her doing, her giving me another chance to fulfill my vow and live out my days in devotion to her.

And so I have spent these long years on this tiny island, in this hut and in the lighthouse tower. She is here, around me, always. In the morning, I hear her voice in the birdsong, and in the evening the breeze carries her soft touch to stroke my cheek. I pray to her each day, three times, and make what small offerings I can on my altar here. The bishop leaves us alone here. No doubt he is sure her worship will die with me.

Sometimes she comes to me—never during the day, not when her enemies bask in the sun and walk the docks and can threaten her—but at night, when it is late, she sometimes comes to me. I will be dreaming, here, in my cot, and in my dream her messenger—a bird, a fish—will wake me and direct me to the narrow beach behind the cabin. So I go out, with my eyes still foggy with heavy sleep, and I sit on a rock. I let my feet dangle in the water, like I am a small boy again.

I feel something nearby, it is moving, I get nervous but I do not move away. Then she jumps out of the water, right next to me, half woman and half fish, and her soft red lips kiss me, and I am transported to paradise.

I have given my life to her. I knew I could never marry a flesh and blood woman. I could not bear the pettiness of a woman's love–have you ever seen how they bicker about whether you have done this chore or that chore? Or their silly rivalries–about how the woman across the way made some cutting remark about your wife's weight or hair, and now you must be indignant about this pointless nonsense too?

She has told me that, when I am ready, I can join with her forevermore. I need only call out to her in prayer and jump into the water. But, she warned me, I must trust her. I should not try to swim or breathe. I must let the embrace of the sea, her sea, pull me under, and let the sea fill up my lungs. Only then will she be ready to take me.

She has not kissed me in some time, but she still visits me in my dreams, telling me I am old, the thread of my life is almost ready to be cut by the gods, and that she has found a new husband. She must mean you, Judah. You have been touched, and blessed. You can rise above the sad muck of your father's life of haggling with ship captains and your mother's bitter moaning about her neighbors.

By this time, the old priest Tobias had ceased to look at Judah, and his eyes were instead fixated on the stars shining in through an open window. Judah stared at his feet and sighed, unsure whether he wanted to wed a goddess–something about eternity and divinity felt too hard and oppressive to him. Was this apparition in the sea a blessing or a curse? Perhaps she was a demon sent to tempt him into disaster. Judah was not sure he wanted the hermit life of old Tobias. Part of his soul wanted the warmth of a real human woman, living on the dry land, and the feeling of being a father to smelly, noisy children tugging at his beard.

Judah looked over again to the hairless, pickled old man: there he lay, smiling ingenuously, utterly sure of the goodness of the gods and the blessedness of his fate. There was something smugly arrogant about that serene hairless head. Why was this old fool so certain he was being led to paradise and that Judah should follow him? Judah grew angry at the self-satisfied old priest, and turned on him:

Tobias, how do you know this siren is not trying to harm you? Haven't you ever heard the sailors' tales of sirens who delight in leading men to jump into the sea to their doom? She wants you to drown yourself–this isn't a goddess, it is a monster, a demon, an ancient, hideous thing bent on toying with us and eating us. How do you know she is not a curse?

Judah's angry words–without him realizing it, his voice had become loud and rough–jolted Tobias out of his reverie:

But how can you say such horrible things? You heard her song and felt her kiss, you know the healing power of her love. Do not spurn that love, or else she will go mad with vengeance upon you. Do not fight this blessing–the goddess's grace is the greatest pleasure you can experience. Let her love you.

Without responding, Judah walked out of the cabin into a refreshingly cool night. Sitting on a rock on the narrow beach, he kicked off his sandals, and let his feet dangle in the sea. At first they were cold, but gradually grew accustomed to the temperature of the water, and soon he could not bear the thought of pulling his feet out again onto dry land. And although he told himself firmly that she was a vicious monster out to drown foolish lonely men, he could not stop himself from hoping the siren would burst forth from the water again and bless him once more with her kiss and her song.

III. Judah's First Betrothal

IT WAS ANOTHER dull evening in the lighthouse, with no ships in sight. It had now been many weeks since he had seen the siren. For days he would long for her, scanning the dark edges of the horizon for a telltale splash or ripple, but then he would tell himself this was madness, the siren would only lead him to be an isolated, miserable recluse like Tobias, or worse. But still, much as there was no happy future chasing sea monsters, that soft kiss …

And no matter how much he paced back and forth in the tower's cramped lookout room, the wild swings between longing and disgust would not leave him be. Exasperated by the monotony of the bare stone walls around him, on a whim Judah raced down the staircase out to a boulder on the beach and shouted incoherently into the distant black sea—a mix of frustration and exuberance.

And then there was something unexpected: an answer echoed back from the sea—a song in Greek. Pivoting quickly towards the sound, he saw her there again. The siren stopped singing, and ran her fingers through her soaked, messy blue hair. The two stared at each other in silence. The siren tilted her head slightly to the side and rocked her body lithely back and forth in the light waves. Judah felt unable either to run away or to swim to her, and so stayed perfectly still. In his mind he fantasized about her kiss, with both of her hands wrapped around his head. And then, in this daydream, she suddenly pulled them both deep under the water.

The siren vanished under the depths once more. Relaxing a bit, Judah looked back at the lighthouse tower and ran his hand slowly over his sparsely-bearded cheek. But soon there was a splash of water on the back of his head and torso. There she was again, next to the rock Judah was sitting upon. Their noses almost touched. Judah could smell her breath, which was lavender and mint. She placed her hands on his temples and gently massaged them. Looking straight into her eyes he was overcome by his conflicting passions and sobbed uncontrollably. The siren calmed him with her singing: songs of pining lovers separated by wars and adventures, of bashful shepherd boys and their hopeless loves for beautiful wood nymphs.

When the siren finished singing she placed a ring, fashioned from red coral, into the palm of Judah's hand, and spoke to him for the first time, in a thickly Greek-accented Latin that was both crystalline and tired: You must decide if I am to be your bride. When you are ready, call me and I will come.

And she disappeared again into the sea.

Judah walked back to the lighthouse, where he hid the ring in his satchel. He was uneasy: to marry a sea monster was to be cursed–somehow–with death or isolation or some other horror of equal measure, an end to his ability to lead an earth-bound human life of wife and children and human warmth. Yet that song, and those indulgent red lips ...

The next morning Judah felt raucously alive at the thrill of waking on dry land in a house filled with the smells of damp laundry and sweat. He could not stop asking excited questions to his parents–about business, about the synagogue, about the neighbors, about anything and everything in the world of the small Jewish community in the sleepy provincial port city. The conversation even lurched toward gossip about new matches and marriage proposals, and Judah suddenly demanded to know thus and such about so many different Jewish girls of marriageable age.

That evening Judah visited Tobias for the first time since their long discussion of the mysterious siren. The old man was swaying gently in his chair, pecking at a small piece of cheese and mumbling hymns to Venus.

Tobias, my apologies for interrupting you. My time here is done, this is my last night at the lighthouse. I must return to the land. This is not my place.

But my son, you must stay here. She needs you. She chose you. Do not leave her alone, she will be sorrowful. She will not let you leave her anyway, you must know that. Do not fight her love.

Judah could not tell if Tobias's eyes were pleading or pitying, but either way, he had to return to a normal human life on the solid mainland. The sea's monstrous apparitions could find new men to torment.

She will be fine without me. If she is an immortal goddess, if she is Venus, then she hardly needs me. If she is a monster, she can feed on someone else.

Judah walked off, feeling triumphant. Enough of this mad old priest and the sea monster who wants to drown them both. He would not be tempted into throwing away real human happiness. Tobias had destroyed his life and his family line, and for what? An occasional fleeting moonlit kiss during the long years of solitude and poverty?

Later that night, pacing along the beach, he had the red coral ring in his hand again, determined to toss it back into the sea—the siren could go scavenge for it at the bottom of the waters, in between whatever slimy creatures squirmed about that far down. Laughing to himself at this image, he then recalled the siren's question about betrothal, and suddenly was inspired with a mischievous prank: he would make the pagan goddess—or sea monster—into a good, earthy Jewish bride, a worthy daughter-in-law to his own bustling, squat, garlic-stained mother.

Judah called out to the sea: Siren, I am ready. But only show me your right hand. No other part of you.

Stifling his laughter, he waded into the nearby shallow water. A moment later up shot a beautiful pale hand.

He grabbed the siren's hand, slipped her ring back on her finger, and intoned in mock seriousness: With this ring you are consecrated unto me according to the laws of Moses and Israel.

Judah released her hand, which immediately disappeared back into the water. Tobias's glorious Venus was now a Jewish bride. The so-called goddess would have to learn how to keep a kosher home on Mount Olympus—indeed, how hard it would be to clean the gods' abode of all the *chametz* piled up over the centuries, so Venus's home could host a proper Passover *seder.* Or lighting the candles to bless the coming of *Shabbat* while making sure Aeolus, lord of the winds, kept a respectful distance. Exploding in wild cackling, he felt he had conquered the beguiling sea monster by making her into an absurd joke, and thereby restored his soul to the hard firm Earth.

IV. Judah's Second Betrothal

AFTER QUITTING THE lighthouse, Judah ended his nocturnal rhythms and began living again in the daylight. He saw now that his nights by the sea had been a brooding a dream world, where everything appeared as shadow and hint and shade—you never saw anything clear and entire. This world of shadows, showing teasing clues of the outline of objects, played tricks on the mind and gave a sense of unreality. But the daytime was brightly lit and straightforward, and there were no patches of darkness blocking one from seeing things as they truly were.

Judah would wander merrily to the taverns by the harbor in the early afternoons, where everyone (himself included) grew rapturously drunk and sailors boasted of truncated romances in different ports around the world. Emboldened by drink one afternoon he asked a group of sailors, who seemed particularly well-traveled, whether any of them had ever seen a siren. They burst into laughter. Their leader, a fat first mate well into middle age, slapped his greasy, callused hand on Judah's shoulder and told him not to be a silly little boy–grown men need women, not made-up fairytale monsters.

His return to the world of grounded reality was completed on a Friday evening shortly after he had grown accustomed once more to the world of daylight. It had been a long time since Judah had attended services in the city's synagogue with his father and brothers. But as dusk fell on that Friday night, and the profane week faded away to make room for holy *Shabbat*, he walked once again to the synagogue with his family. Inside were tables around which the different Jewish families clustered for prayer. The walls were decorated with pictures from the life of Abraham, reflecting the obsession of the wealthy merchant who had last paid to renovate the building with the stories and legends of the first patriarch. On the wall near Judah's family was the young Abraham in his father's shop in Chaldea, smashing the idols of the false gods, while across the room Sodom and Gomorrah smoldered in just punishment. Amidst the densely packed benches around his family's table, Judah's small nephew, who had just recently mastered walking without falling on his face, scrambled under and around the table legs and popped up more than once, giggling, onto Judah's knee. His childish face filled Judah with warmth, and he pinched the child's cheeks and rubbed the top of his head.

The Hebrew chants lifted Judah's spirits, filling him with memories of home–of fresh-baked cakes, and games with his brothers in their courtyard, and his mother stroking him while he lay sick in bed. Judah thought: This is where real life is lived. Father Abraham was right. Smash the idols of false gods, phantoms of absurd nighttime visions, and live your life boldly in the daylight.

After the *Shabbat* ended, the family discussed what Judah should do now. He wanted to work in the family business, but far from the sea. This irritated his father–after so much time in the lighthouse, who would know the ships and the harbor better than Judah? Couldn't he at least put some of that knowledge to work?

But Judah angrily refused–he was done with the sea, he was never going back, he wanted a life on land and land alone.

Calm down, calm down, his father replied. Hire a wagon and driver and go into the countryside on Monday. We need to buy skins and salted meats to sell. Make the rounds of the farmers and estates in the interior.

So Judah became the family's buyer in the settlements and estates of the interior. He often spent most of the week traveling from farm to farm, staying at inns and haggling with the peasants and landowners, as he slowly learned how to tell good hides from bad ones, and which honey had real value, and what meat was ready to spoil.

While Judah was away inspecting hides in the countryside, Tobias's body was found one morning washed up on the docks of the harbor, clearly a victim of drowning, although his face was frozen in an eerily beatific smile. No one was entirely sure what to do with his corpse, as neither of the two communities with burial societies–the Christians and the Jews–could lay claim to him. So the body sat there, rotting and stinking, in the offices of the municipal administration until the imperial bureaucrats lost their patience and paid a farmer from the interior to deposit the corpse on a mountain where, so the rumor went, there was still a crumbling shrine to the almost forgotten goddess Venus. When he later heard of these events, Judah refused to think much about his old friend's demise, as he had, by then, long willed himself to ignore the sea and its gods and monsters.

Once Judah was firmly established in the family business and the community became confident that his eccentric phase had ended, there was a concerted effort to find him a wife. While he tramped about in search of merchandise, his parents made discrete inquiries among the city's Jewish families about eligible brides.

One Friday night, after returning from synagogue, Judah sat down to dinner at his parents' house with a new guest seated at his left: a woman slightly younger than himself, with long brown curly hair and a busty, curvy figure, named Rivkah, the eldest daughter of one of the city's tavern-owners. She helped her father serve drinks and clean tables, and a lifetime of being around drunken sailors and foolish boasting had left her skeptical of anything she could not grab and smell and beat with her own two hands. That night, though, she appeared to be ill at ease. Her mother, who sat to her other side, nudged her to speak to Judah. But Rivkah stammered and blushed.

He tried to help her relax: Do you like the fish? My mother is using a new seasoning, something someone in the market told her was both spicy and sweet. Do you think it worked?

Rivkah stared down at the plate, neither eating nor looking at Judah.

His voice fell into a conspiratorial whisper: I am not so sure. The fish seems dry and bland to me. But I do not want to upset my mother, she worked so hard on the meal, she so wants us all to be happy. So I smile thankfully at her while I chew her tasteless cooking.

Rivkah ran two fingers through her hair and stifled a giggle. Although she still did not look up, Judah was sure she had smiled. *She agrees,* he thought, *she knows the fish should be cooked better. We share a little secret together now. That is a beginning.*

Feeling emboldened Judah raised his voice again:

I spend almost all of the week buying and selling in the countryside. There is a lovely inn a few hours' wagon ride from here, in a small village, where I often stay. The innkeeper is always telling me how worried he is about his daughter. What will happen to her, he sighs, all these men come through, drink my wine, and then try to tempt her virtue. Who knows, he likes to say, one day she will run off with a handsome drunk and I will never see her again. At least not before the lout has run through all the coins he has stolen from my purse.

And when I came to that inn this week, and did not see the innkeeper's daughter, I feared fate had dealt cruelly with the old man. But then I saw he was happy. Why? I asked. Because, said the innkeeper, my daughter wed a farmer's son. She realized her happiness would be with a good local boy, not some wandering braggart who promises riches and delights beyond compare.

Rivkah was now looking at Judah. Your friend sounds like my father, she said. All tavern-keeping and inn-keeping fathers must be in some secret society where they plot their daughters' fates.

Have you ever been tempted to run off with a drunken braggart, maybe hop into his ship and see where the wind goes?

Rivkah flashed a mischievous smile.

Well, none of them have been handsome enough yet. And the last thing a girl wants is to run off with a drunk. A man who cannot even stand up, or stop urinating all over himself, is hardly in a position to whisk a girl away on a romantic voyage.

Have you met any fine farmers' lads yet?

Rivkah smiled more broadly. I am trying. Maybe there is one at dinner tonight.

Maybe I need to settle down with a farm, Judah volleyed back. He was enjoying the back and forth, although he was far from infatuated with Rivkah. Rather, she made him feel comfortable: a solid helpmeet in this world, a possible partner in the task of building a household. She did not set his pulse racing, and for that he was grateful. This is what Tobias failed to grasp, he realized, that happiness lies in cozy domestic comfort, not divine ecstasy.

After dinner, Judah escorted Rivkah home, with her mother trailing behind at a respectable distance. Judah and Rivkah spoke of their dreams—dreams blander than the fish: the routines of a settled marriage with many children and lazy long naps on Saturday afternoons. Judah laughed with genuine affection at how well-matched they were in their dullness.

No, Rivkah countered, it is not dullness, it is what life should be about: marriage, children, obeying the commandments of the Holy One, living a complete Jewish life. Maybe we can do that together.

Judah looked away and sighed. They had reached Rivkah's door, and should have ended the evening with appropriately polite and endearingly awkward goodnights. But Judah was seized instead by a strange impulse:

Rivkah, he asked, what would you think if you saw a siren, half woman, half fish, jump out of the sea during a thunderstorm? Would you believe it? Would you want to speak to her? Or drive her away? Or run away yourself? What would you do?

She responded at first with a baffled stare, but when, after several moments, it became clear that Judah really wanted a reply, she finally said, with the calm authority she might use with a misbehaving little boy, that she had never thought much about sea monsters, but would probably tell the siren to go return to her storybook. Or maybe to devour the drunken sailors before they started throwing cups and pitchers at one another in her father's tavern, which she would be stuck cleaning up.

Judah fell silent. Her breezy certainty left him feeling, to his own surprise, suddenly quite melancholy, as if the world had been drained of its capacity for pleasure. As he brooded, the three of them—Judah, Rivkah, and Rivkah's mother—stood silently outside Rivkah's door. Rivkah and her mother locked eyes with one another.

Don't mind me, he said quickly after noticing their concerned stares, I sometimes have silly daydreams. Well, it was lovely speaking tonight. I hope we will speak again soon. Have a good evening, and a good *Shabbat* rest.

A visibly relieved Rivkah wished him a good night.

Judah detoured on his walk home to stroll near the harbor. One of the ships docked nearby had a wooden sculpture of a siren on the prow. Judah walked closer to her, and saw that her paint was peeling and one of her eyes seemed to be chipped off. The broken siren flooded him with sorrow, and, as he stroked her gently, tears lightly trickled down Judah's cheeks.

For a moment, he was certain Rivkah had committed a grave crime upon this siren's person and hated her.

But soon he stepped back, wiped away the tears, and steadied himself. It was not so bad that the world was dull and limited. Tobias had lived his life as a great divine drama, some sort of lunatic Greek tragedy, and look at his pitiful fate. Tobias could have used a Rivkah—a sensible Jewish girl with her feet on solid land to tell him to stop being ridiculous and to go buy some fresh chicken for dinner and to get the children's shoes mended. No more dreams of goddesses on the waves, there was too much to be done in the house and not enough time in the day. Girls like Rivkah saved you from throwing away real life, with its real—even if bland—pleasures, for lurid hallucinations.

Over the next several weeks, Rivkah became a regular guest at Judah's family dinners, at first with her mother but later alone. This became the highlight of Judah's week. As he went around the villages in the countryside, he mentally took note of news and anecdotes that he would pass on to Rivkah: updates about the harvest, odd facts about what cows and horses prefer to eat, or discussions of the way the weather was trending—the various villagers had strong views on the meaning of different clouds.

On Friday nights, after returning from synagogue, Judah would anxiously watch the door, as no one ever told him beforehand whether Rivkah was expected and he was too ashamed—although he could not explain why—simply to ask. But then the door would creak open slightly, hesitantly, and Rivkah would shuffle in and greet Judah's mother with a jug of wine. His mother would thank her profusely for her kind gift and, of course, Rivkah was welcome to join them. Rivkah would then matter-of-factly find her way to her customary seat next to Judah.

The conversation would usually begin slowly. He would ask her, stiffly, how her week had been. Rivkah, who had been sitting still, with her hands folded on her lap and her eyes aimed at her kneecaps, would suddenly come to life. The focus of her week had been buying wine and mead for the family tavern. Prices, she would explain, were moving such and so, and supply was this and quality was that, all a result of a shortage created by a great landowner in the interior buying all the best barrels at excessive cost in anticipation of a sumptuous banquet. Her father was always annoyed at first with the results of her purchases—every price was too high for what he swore was weak alcohol with a sour taste—but once Rivkah had patiently explained the constraints she was under her father would grudgingly approve of her efforts.

By this time, the soup would have been cleared and the fish would be passed around as the hostess poured out second and third cups of wine. Rivkah would tear a piece of bread to dip into the tasteless fish sauce, and her intense, loud chewing sometimes caused her words to slur and jumble a bit.

With her belly mostly full, Rivkah would now describe how busy the tavern was. And no matter how few sailors passed through, there was always, always, a brawl to be described. Yet Rivkah had a sensible approach to these fights. Their causes or objects were irrelevant and, in fact, usually either inscrutable or a comically inane instance of wounded self-regard. What mattered instead was the amount of time that it eventually took her father to relocate the fight outside the tavern (Rivkah was indifferent to what happened after the brawlers were out of her eyesight), and how many items had been broken, thrown, or disfigured; fights were judged by the degree of clean-up required afterwards. She would often profess herself baffled that so many grown men wanted to spend their precious leisure time hurling tables and cups and pitchers at one another's heads.

It was all that time in the sea, she would muse, that somehow made these men lose their wits. Locals never started fights, she would continue, only sailors whose ships had docked at the port. This was why she would never marry a man who had anything to do with the sea—she was sure that, no matter how nice he may seem, he was secretly mad and violent. Rivkah often praised Judah's wisdom in keeping his business affairs on the firm, sensible soil of the land.

This was Judah's cue to speak. The honey cakes and mead would now be making their way around the table. As Rivkah shoveled several slices of cake into her mouth, he would recount the highlights of his week: the harvest was looking good or bad, there was a disease in so-and-so's flock of sheep, or a bad storm had damaged the huts of a couple of villagers, and he gave a detailed report of how their dwellings were being repaired.

There were carefully prescribed, if unspoken, limits to this verbal dance. Human bodies were a taboo subject. While Judah reported in minute detail as to the health and reproductive vigor of every flock of animals he encountered, neither he nor Rivkah ever mentioned the illnesses of people around them, much less anyone's reproductive vigor or lack thereof. Nor, as polite young unmarried Jews, did they ever touch or kiss. Judah thought of his relations with Rivkah as decent and correct, a hard won equanimity that was a relief, and a reassurance he had avoided Tobias's awful fate.

After dinner, Judah would escort Rivkah home. These walks were often silent, punctuated only by halting, forced comments about the chores each had to do once *Shabbat* ended the next evening. As at dinner, they were scrupulous in their efforts to keep their bodies apart. Yet sometimes, during these quiet walks, his eyes would wander across to the harbor and then just a tad farther to the old lighthouse, and he would be seized with a terrible, inchoate longing for a different life. But he willed himself to suppress these urges.

He knew what was expected of him, which Rivkah's eyes—now hopeful, now impatient—kept signaling: she wanted him to arrange for his father to ask her father to betroth her to him. After all, they had, with appropriate modesty, taken the time to become acquainted and to confirm their fitness as a marriage match. It was time to move on to the next step.

Rivkah would never say as much directly. But she would tell her foot-dragging suitor tales of recent betrothals of other Jews their age, or, every so often, she would heave and sigh about the fate of some poor old maid who had died alone and childless, because no man had been willing to wed her. Judah would not reply to these stories, but would stare off to the sea and try hard not to follow her meaning. The sound of the waves crashing gently against the surf and receding back again emptied his mind of all concern. The dry land had suddenly seemed an uncomfortable place to be.

His parents too appeared to be anxious about the inexplicable delay in Judah declaring his intentions. His mother dropped all sorts of little hints, about what she had been like as a blushing bride twirling with nervous energy, in many ways so like Rivkah. Or Judah's house would echo with anecdotes about his brothers' weddings and good-hearted jokes about how Judah would look in their wedding clothes.

Yet Judah could not bring himself to take the fateful step, even though he knew it was what he should do, and what everyone was waiting for him to do. The case for marrying Rivkah should have been compelling: she was level-headed, wise, and determined to assemble a teeming Jewish household of her own–just the wife Judah told himself he should want. He knew he had been blessed with the perfect match, but it all seemed to be colored in grey. The lights of the Sun and the Moon dimmed in the presence of her earnestly respectable tedium. She was a comfort to a tired young man who had exhausted himself hauling wagons about the countryside, but like a soft, worn couch she lulled one into drowsy detachment rather than passion. He was scared of spending his whole life in a stuffy little house with his eyelids heavy from too many helpings of bland, stale *challah*.

One Thursday morning, Judah had unexpectedly completed his rounds already for the week, and so was able to return home earlier than usual. His father took advantage of this opportunity to pull him aside for a private discussion.

Judah, he said, I cannot help noticing how fond you are of talking to Rivkah, the tavern keeper's daughter.

His father paused expectantly, but Judah said nothing and merely looked at his feet. So his father continued:

I cannot fault you. She is a good girl, the kind of girl who makes a good wife–not too flighty. Now a sensible unmarried Jewish girl does not spend this much time with an unmarried

Jewish boy without expecting a betrothal. It would be unfair for the boy to give her false hope and to keep her from other possible matches, if he were not truly serious. So, are you serious, Judah? If so, I will approach her father and negotiate terms. If not, let the girl move on. It is not right to let her become an old maid vainly hoping for some foolish man to grow up and accept his place as a Jewish husband and father. So what will it be?

Judah was even less comfortable now. Everything was moving too rapidly. His father was right, he knew that, and he agreed he should want Rivkah as his wife. But not just yet. Life was in a good rhythm, safe and easy and predictable. Still, he knew Rivkah and her family expected a marriage proposal, and it would hurt her deeply if he were not to request a formal betrothal.

Unable to think of a reason to delay, and too ashamed to outright refuse, Judah felt compelled to ask his father to approach Rivkah's father to negotiate the terms of the engagement. Judah's father was overjoyed, and a tear slid down from his eye into his bushy beard.

Having at last given in to everyone's expectations, Judah now felt quite relieved, and even proud of himself: he was bringing joy to his parents, and to Rivkah, doing the right thing and starting his own Jewish family. In his self-satisfied daydream he was leading a Passover *seder* with his little sons gathered around him in the flickering candlelight, telling them the story of the exodus from Egypt as they sat in rapt, obedient attention at the feet of his soft, worn couch.

Once the betrothal agreement was executed shortly thereafter, Judah felt an urge he could not explain to hear Rivkah sing. During their initial courtship, he had had no occasion to listen to her sing, which did not trouble him, as he had been taken with the steely, matter of fact determination with which she tackled life's everyday nuisances. But now he longed for a song.

Returning one afternoon from his rounds in the countryside, he passed a well where the girls from the outlying farms had queued up to draw water. This was no easy labor: many of them seemed prematurely bent from the heavy work of loading and hauling, and their faces twisted in pain as they trudged their full buckets home.

Nevertheless, at that moment, three girls in the line, whom Judah guessed must have been sisters, or at least friends, put down their buckets and began to clap in unison, in some kind of rhythm. After they found their beat, they started to sing a rousing song, not beautiful, but fast and catchy. Judah found himself stopping and tapping his foot in time to the cheerful tune. The girls noticed him, and laughed, and sang all the louder. While their singing did not have the siren's bewitching melancholy beauty, it made his pulse race with joy.

That night, over *Shabbat* dinner, he relayed this anecdote to Rivkah, and, with a foolish grin on his face, banged the table to mimic the rhythm of the song, even singing the one verse he recalled. But she wrinkled her brow and folded her arms: You need to pay less heed to loose Gentile women and their songs. It is not right for girls to make such a spectacle of themselves.

But it was only a song, Judah protested, where can be the harm in that? You must love some songs, right? When you sweep up the mess in the tavern, don't you hum a little something to yourself?

There is real harm in their behavior. Girls' voices singing catchy songs lead men's thoughts in improper directions. Look at how you stopped paying attention to your actual business and gawked like a drunken buffoon. It is a good thing they were simple country girls having a bit of fun with you, and not–may it never happen to us–demons like Lilith come to seduce you into sin. Your weakness for pretty songs will lose you this world and the world to come if you are not careful.

Judah wiggled in his seat, feeling guilty, although he told himself he had no reason to. Still, determined to show Rivkah there was merit in song, he rallied once more:

But you didn't answer my question. Don't you hum some song or other to yourself as you work, even if ever so softly?

I do not.

Judah changed the subject to the recent increase in the price of fresh fish. Rivkah needed little prodding here, and launched into an extended monotone ballad of her woes in buying fish for the tavern's famed fish stews, prepared by her mother fresh each day, and a favorite of sailors of all nationalities. The thought of burying the once wild, dancing sea creatures in scalding garlic broths delighted her.

Yet he could not shake the nagging desire to hear his fiancée sing. She told him he was being a fool. Why did he need to hear her sing? Would that satisfy him that she would be a good mother? That she could be trusted with the household finances? What was the point?

But he would not let go of this fixation. Finally, one night, when Judah brought Rivkah home from dinner, her resistance crumbled. If this is so important to you, she said, then fine, I will sing. I do not want to spend the rest of my life hounded by my husband with this stupid request.

Rivkah closed her eyes, took a deep breath, and sang a tune in Greek that was some kind of a sailor's song–something, as best Judah could make out, about a drunken captain vomiting all over the deck. Regardless of the words, Rivkah's voice sounded horrible: screeching, hoarse, tone deaf. She reminded him of a wailing, sickly goat.

Satisfied now?

Judah silently nodded his assent, and never asked her to sing again.

V. The Murder

THE WEDDING CEREMONY was fittingly solemn, and Judah felt truly moved as his bride circled him seven times. Although her movements were clumsy (she repeatedly stepped on and dirtied the hem of her gown), he saw this as a sign of real love and devotion. Human women, he thought, can never move with the perfect grace of a goddess, but that gift of awkwardness made them worth loving, and was proof they loved you in turn–love sparkled most brightly in embarrassed, lowered eyes.

Then the joyous reception followed. On the tables were heaps of delicacies, spiced meats, fruits, nuts and pastries. The wedding jester was dazzling: he swallowed swords, ate fire, juggled a half dozen balls, and made sly jokes throughout about his own supposedly feeble skills and how his wife henpecked him. Judah, well primed with copious amounts of wine, swooned with delight.

The city's entire small Jewish community had come, as well as many out of town relatives. There were even a smattering of

Christian dignitaries–the Bishop's personal secretary (his holiness was forced by church business to attend a synod somewhere or other to the East, as there was, alas, always a new heresy to address), a couple of local landowners with commercial ties to Judah's family, and various imperial functionaries billeted to the dull provincial town, who needed to while away the time before they could return again to the luxury and sophistication of Antioch or Constantinople. The festive wedding provided much needed relief from the boredom of enforcing customs duties at the harbor.

Once the wedding jester had finished his performance, the guests dug into the heaping platters on the tables before them. But Judah had little opportunity to indulge himself, as guest after guest approached to congratulate him on his fine marriage and excellent match. The bride's good sense and shrewd wits were praised to the skies, and everyone marveled at the amazing variety and abundance of delicious food. Bombarded by one puffy half-drunk face after another, moist palms gripping his hands and shoulders, Judah could only repeat the same two or three shopworn phrases of humble gratitude.

The celebrations lasted late into the evening, and there were many raucous toasts–after all, the bride's family did own a tavern and had something of an expertise in that sort of thing. Judah was obliged to stand, wave, smile, and imbibe fully each time, leaving him so drunk that by the end of the evening he could barely stand.

Still, tradition demanded he enter his wife's bridal bed that night to consummate the marriage. When the celebrations had at last petered out, Judah stumbled into bed next to Rivkah, praying silently for the strength not to vomit all over his new bride as he had to contend with not only the excess of wine in his belly, but also the sickly sweet smell of her excessively applied perfume.

Judah's eyes welled with tears when he saw Rivkah's hopeful, nervous smile and felt her soft, plump flesh press against him. At that moment, she seemed to him the most beautiful woman in the world, and with all his strength he grabbed her head and kissed her.

This was Judah's first kiss since his embrace of the siren, but the two kisses could not have been more different. The siren's kiss suspended awareness of time and the surrounding world, luring his soul into the vastness of the sea. Rivkah's kiss was very much in the present: he could feel her hot breath and food-speckled teeth and eager twitching.

After the kiss, Judah peeled off his sweat-soaked robe to lay naked next to his wife, slipping his leg between her two legs, reveling in her nightgown's softness, and placing his arms around Rivkah so that his chest pressed gently against her breasts. Nevertheless, all that drink had enfeebled him to the point that he could not perform his conjugal duties.

Never mind, he told himself in his dull haze, they had a lifetime of nights together, and he had no plans ever to be this drunk again. Fitted naturally together in this tight embrace, the couple drifted to sleep in absolute peace and security.

Judah awoke in the morning with a pounding headache, and a fresh attack of nausea. During the course of the night, the two newlyweds had come so unraveled that he now found himself at the far end of the bed away from Rivkah, who seemed to be asleep still. He went outside into the harsh sunlight to draw water from the nearby well, part of which he drank and part of which he tossed over his head to knock the drowsiness out of him.

After walking to the harbor, he crouched down on a small dock, and dangled his feet in the sea. Today was the beginning of his life as a man with a family. Soon he would be a father, he was certain of it, and he would walk to these shores with his children, where they would hunt for stray seashells and chase the birds.

But the sweet daydream was cut short when, a few moments later, a multitude of hands grabbed Judah and pulled him up. There were confused shouts all around. Judah could make no sense of what was going on, but he felt himself jostled and shoved as the crowd traveled back toward his house again.

The house was encircled by mayhem: women were moaning and screaming and tearing their hair, and Judah's father paced nervously about, visibly straining to maintain a posture of calm strength. When he saw Judah standing dazed in the crowd he pulled his son over to the side and then into the house, through a hallway somehow suddenly full of strange wailing people and into an empty bedroom.

Although the two men were now alone, Judah's father resumed his silent pacing. Judah demanded to know what was going on and where was Rivkah—no doubt she could explain all this madness and restore some order.

You really do not know then, do you?

What is there to know?

Who can say why such things happen? That is right, you left early this morning, so someone said, so you would not know. The Holy One, Blessed be He, in His Righteous Judgment, has taken Rivkah back to His bosom and brought her to Paradise in the World to Come. The burial society will clean the body, and the funeral will be tomorrow. Say *kaddish* for her soul, Judah.

Father, this is absurd. How can Rivkah be dead? She is young, she is healthy.

It was witchcraft. When Rivkah had not woken for the longest time your mother went into her room to fetch her for breakfast. But Rivkah was dead. There were no marks on her body, no cuts, no lesions. So how did she die? She drowned. Her chest and throat and mouth were filled with water—and not well water or river water, but saltwater from the sea, with bits of seaweed and red coral. Yet how can a girl drown in her bed on dry land? It can only be witchcraft. We must honor and mourn for Rivkah, but be careful, something evil is afoot, and it is close to us.

Judah jumped to his feet.

Stop it! This is madness. This cannot be. People do not drown in their beds, and there are no witches stalking us.

Judah's father sighed, shook his head, and then motioned for Judah to follow him again. The two men went back into the crowded hallway and shoved their way into what had been the couple's new bedroom.

Go look.

The bed was empty except for some rumpled sheets and blankets. Looking around Judah saw two men diligently working on the floor. And there she was, lying between these two men on the floor, his beloved, his bride. Her body was naked, and stiff and being carefully scrubbed clean for burial. Judah looked into her eyes, but saw nothing looking back at him. Judah bent down and kissed her cold cheek, causing her mouth to open and emit an overpowering stench of sea salt. A moment later a jet of dank salt water burst from her mouth onto Judah's head.

He pushed his way out of the room and back into the street. Paying no more attention to the moaning and gossiping crowds, he ran through the cobblestone streets and alleyways, past stalls, colliding with barrels and crates and picking himself up again, until he reached the synagogue.

It was empty. Judah ran to the raised dais, the *bimah*, and up to the broad wooden ark holding the community's Torah scrolls, where he collapsed into a tight ball on the ground and sobbed. In between his moans he recited the *kaddish* as best he could and begged the Righteous Judge to treat Rivkah with kindness and mercy.

During the prescribed period of mourning, there were prayer services in his house each evening where the many guests urged him to remember that, beneath the apparent inexplicable tragedy, lay the Holy One's ultimate plan, which must always be good and just. While our limited human perception cannot grasp matters fully, he was told many times, trust that the Righteous Judge has done what is for the best. Judah nodded mutely in response, but felt only an enveloping numbness in his limbs. The loud chattering voices were grating, but he lacked the will to shoo them away.

Other visitors, especially imperial officials, were less sure of the ultimate goodness of events, and from them Judah learned, bit by bit, about the official inquiry into Rivkah's death:

Judah's father was not alone in suspecting witchcraft in this most unusual case of drowning on dry land. Rivkah's parents had the same intuition of foul play, and demanded that the authorities investigate. The local church authorities also pushed for a prompt inquiry into the causes of death, including any role played by witchcraft. Although the bishop was still away, his secretary was a sharp student of the dangers of black magic and occult practices, and he was convinced there were hidden conclaves of demon-worshipping pagans, obstinate acolytes of Tobias's old creed, who were bent on vengeance for the desecration of the goddess Venus's temple so many years ago and the triumph of the true faith.

The bishop's secretary had been attempting to track these conclaves of secret enemies for some time. His inquiries had led him to an old woman who lived alone in the nearby woods. Farmers and other country people would visit her when family members became ill, as she trafficked in amulets, herbs, potions, and other unholy remedies. The bishop's secretary was convinced this was the devil's trap: make people sick and then have his wicked disciple magically cure the illness, weakening faith in true revelation and encouraging belief in heresy.

And now, he asserted, this witch had gone too far. For reasons unclear at that moment, the witch had chosen to murder a Jewish bride on her wedding night. This must, the secretary insisted, be some type of sacrifice to appease, or to goad, the foul powers of Hell.

Based upon the secretary's testimony, and for lack of a better alternative, the imperial officials took the old woman into custody. She denied any role in the Jewish girl's death. Nevertheless, the imperial officials in charge of the investigation were confident that, given enough time and beatings, she would confess the truth and be duly executed, putting a crisp conclusion to the unsettling incident.

Judah listened but felt unable to care. Beating and harassing old women in the forest would not resurrect his Rivkah. He felt utterly adrift. Everything in his life had been fitting together so neatly: business, wife, soon children and a home of his own. He was to be a solid Jewish householder–shrewd but honest in business, a caring but stern and wise father and husband at home. Yet now it was all gone.

After the period of mourning ended, Judah avoided the city. Its narrow grey cobblestone streets and rundown taverns filled his soul with sadness and longing, as around each corner he thought he could spy Rivkah walking in the corner of his eye. At night, he would find himself calling out to her, and sleep evaded him even though he was tortured by a fatigue he could not shake off.

So he fled to the countryside, only returning for *Shabbat*, and sometimes not even then. When there was no more business to transact, he would store his belongings with a trusted innkeeper and wander in the forest, where, completely alone in the dense foliage, he was able to empty his mind and enjoy the scents of the wild flowers and fruit trees.

VI. The Flight

THE INNKEEPER GREETED Judah with only a grumble and a nod. After pouring some wine for him and laying out a hunk of black bread, the big barrel of a man and his wife retreated into a corner to exchange heated whispers. Judah grew uneasy as the two cast worried glances at him. Had he somehow fallen out of favor with the local landowner? Maybe someone in the area had started agitating against the Jews as happened from time to time? Who knew? But whatever it was, it was something ill.

Judah had often frequented this inn, performing small favors now and again for the innkeeper, such as secretly restocking the inn's supplies of various goods at deeply discounted prices that would have upset his father. But it was important to have friends in the isolated, rough patches of the countryside, and this innkeeper had always been a good friend. The two men liked to sit together on the small inn's veranda, watching the sunset and sharing a bottle of wine.

When Judah's cup was mostly drained, the innkeeper sat down next to him at the wood table. Judah gestured to offer to share his wine.

The innkeeper lowered his head and knitted his brow, speaking in a conspiratorial whisper:

Listen, Judah, now is not the time for drinking wine. You must not know what has happened. The governor's men and the bishop's men are out looking for you, and mean to arrest you. I am only telling you this as you have been a good friend, and I can only help you now, before anyone learns that you came here. But you need to run. Into the forest.

But why? What crime could I have committed?

The innkeeper sighed and shook his head slowly.

It is a bad business when witches get up to no good. You recall the witch they arrested for your wife's murder? Well, according to what I heard from the landowner's men who have been to town, the crazy old hag finally stopped ranting curses and spells at the soldiers—which even she saw did her no good— and started to talk. She says she had a vision where a siren rose from the harbor to drown Rivkah in her bed with evil magic. And then here is where you come in: the witch says the siren did this in a jealous rage because you are her lover.

Now, I may be off on the details, you see these are just bits and scraps of rumor. But it does not really matter. It is a fact that armed men are riding in formation in the country roads looking for you, to arrest you and beat you and ask their crazy questions. I know you are a good man, and I know you loved your wife, so I think there is some mix up. But once they start with the beatings and the tortures, a man will confess to anything to make it stop. So run, run now, get out of here as fast as you can.

Judah sat in silence, unable to speak or move. This cannot be happening to me, he thought. Who could believe I would harm my Rivkah? Maybe I will talk to them and show them the truth of the matter.

But then Judah thought further: what if someone had seen him kiss the siren? Or place a ring upon her finger? He was sure no one had been about on those desolate nights, but could he ever truly be certain? Not to mention old Tobias. Who knows what that old man may have said in his last days about the siren or Judah?

Get out! Go, now, quick! No telling when they will get here.

The innkeeper's words, suddenly much louder, woke Judah from his stupor. He thanked his old friend and told him to help himself to the contents of his wagon in the courtyard— that abundant pile of hides and cheeses would be more than enough recompense for the innkeeper's good deed.

After unhitching his horse, Judah rode without stopping until dusk, through the quiet, empty forest with its monoto- nous scenery. As the sun set he rested for a quick meal, unsure where he was, but hopeful that he had traveled some distance from his pursuers. Ahead was an endless expanse of the same road through the same forest. Realizing his pursuers would no doubt learn he had gone this way and overtake him, he decided it was best to leave the highway and the horse and go by foot into the woods.

The sun set fast in the forest, as the thick web of leaves and branches overhead blocked virtually all light from the sky.

With no idea in what direction he was heading, Judah walked slowly in the dark, groping ahead with his hands. Every rustling sound—a squirrel scrambling up a tree, a bird suddenly taking off—made him freeze in terror.

At last, there was a clearing where the full yellow moon shone brightly upon the meadow. Exhaustion finally caught up with Judah, and he collapsed into a deep slumber on the grass and dirt. In his dream, he was floating in a rickety dinghy on the open sea under the same full yellow moon. Rivkah was with him. They talked again of their plans for children, and as each child was discussed and named—here a Dovid, there a Sarah, now a Yitzhak—that child would appear on the boat and sit at the happy couple's feet. Judah worried aloud about whether such a flimsy vessel could hold the weight of so many people, but Rivkah told him to put his trust in the Holy One, Blessed be He.

Then there was a splash, and up surged the siren, with her blue hair and blue eyes, her red lips and red coral necklace, towering over the cramped little boat adrift in the desolate sea. As she looked down upon Judah and his family, she calmly picked up one child after another, and ate them all. The children did not complain or resist, but meekly submitted to her will with glassy eyes and blank expressions. Judah felt paralyzed by fear.

But Rivkah fought for her children, biting the siren's fingers and moving her children behind her. The siren pulled Rivkah close, eye-to-eye, yet Rivkah held steadfast: Monster, animal, give me back my babies, the Holy One will punish you severely for your great crimes.

The siren's face twisted with hate. It was now her turn: Thieving whore, you took what is mine.

And she plunged Rivkah's head into the sea until she drowned, and then let the dead body float away upon the glassy grey-black sea.

Judah woke with a start. The sun was high in the sky. Soon he was groping forward again in the dense forest, but everywhere were the same tall, thick trees and the same roof of green leaves, and there was no way to be certain that he was not merely running foolishly in circles.

Something wet hit his forehead, at first only a couple of drops, but soon there was a raging downpour from the dark clouds overhead. Judah looked around frantically but saw no shelter. The rain poured down relentlessly, and it became difficult to see. In his panic and confusion he tripped on a fallen branch, landing at an angle, in terrible pain. His ankle was on fire, but he could not move it.

With great effort and shooting pains throughout his immobile leg, he maneuvered his torso up and against a nearby tree trunk. But the strain exhausted him. Placing his satchel above his head, Judah could no longer keep his eyes open.

Time melted away as the puddles and the mud crept ever higher. The water laid siege to Judah's shoes, soaking them thoroughly on the outside, then seeking and finding small weaknesses in the leather's defenses, into which the invading water droplets poured their icy wetness directly onto the skin of his feet. The ground was giving way under the pressure of his weight, and dirty rivulets from the puddles crept up Judah's calves and knees.

Judah thought of Rivkah's frightful death, of the evil sorcery that had made her drown in her own bed, and shuddered as to what curse or spell had been cast upon him now. Shivering violently, delirium overtook him: There he saw Rivkah, as she was on their wedding day, and now the synagogue, on Yom Kippur, as the men beat their breasts in agonized guilt over their sins and begged the Holy One, Blessed be He, to be permitted another year of life on this Earth with their families.

Next in his hallucinations, it was a calm night on the sea, and he saw an immense, brightly colored fish. No, the fish was not a fish. The bottom half was a fish, with a shiny tail, but the top half was a woman with blue hair and red lips. After leaping in the air, she bent down so her massive head faced Judah's alarmed, twitching face, and she showed him her ring.

We wed, under the sacred laws of your Torah, and you betrayed me. But we will be together again soon, for eternity. Rest, rest, close your eyes, and rest. I will never let you betray our marriage again. Rest, sweet husband, and let the water cradle you.

Judah awoke in the corner of a wide room, naked but dry under a rough wool blanket. There was a fire nearby, and its warmth felt good. The sun shined in through the hut's open door. Sitting up he was able to move his ankle slightly, although not without searing pain shooting through his leg.

Deciding it was better to rest his ankle and reassuring himself that he must be somewhere safe—some kindly soul had to have brought him here—Judah sat half-upright, covered by the blanket, as the light from the door faded from bright yellow to pink to purple. When the day was about to end, in walked a short, round woman with masses of grey-brown hair wrapped in a bun on top of her head. Her dress was stained and slightly ripped at the bottom. Judah thought she appeared to be towards the later years of middle age.

The woman gave a start:

You scared me, young man. I did not realize you were up. You were awful sick when I found you in the forest, and you're lucky I found you. You did not have much longer. But a good warm fire brought you back. Now tell me, what is your name, son? Where are you from?

Judah remained alert enough to recall that he was a fugitive. He needed an alias–something Jewish, he thought, since she has seen my nakedness and knows I am a Jew from the mark of the covenant of Abraham on my body.

Yes, sorry, you asked my name, I am still not quite myself. It is Reuven. I am a traveler. I became lost in the forest. Where are we now? How did you find me?

Well, Reuven, it is a pleasure to be formally introduced. I am Julia, and this is my humble abode in the very same forest. I was running home in the downpour–where that came from, the gods only know, we never get storms like that–trying to get home–I had been out picking berries–and I tripped over something on the ground, near to my home here, and that something was you. You were shivering and screaming about your ring and some giant fish. Anyways, I could not leave you there to die, now could I? So I dragged you over here and hung your clothes to dry inside. Lay you down under a thick blanket. And waited and waited. But now you have come around again. Are you still hurt? Can you move everything?

My ankle–and Judah stretched his leg to show his wounded ankle, tried to wiggle it, but let out a horrible moan.

Not too fast, not too fast yet, my new friend, Reuven. You may need to be my guest a bit longer. Rest, let it heal. Let me get you something for that pain.

Julia heated a small pot of water over the fire, into which she dropped a few dry leaves and wrinkled berries, gently rocking the pot to mix the ingredients together. When she judged the potion to be ready, she held his chin with one hand while pouring the liquid into his mouth with the other. The hot drink felt soothing in his dry throat. Soon Judah's head and limbs felt heavy, and he lay down again on his back, staring at the hut's ceiling as he slowly fell asleep.

When Judah woke the next morning he felt a surge of energy, and his ankle no longer hurt. He jumped to his feet–and, distracted by the thrill of his newfound health, did not notice he was naked in the sunlight. Julia giggled like a young girl.

It works every time, dear Reuven, that remedy puts you to sleep and does all the healing work. Better than any physician, and much cheaper too. But you need some clothes. Over there–she pointed to a pile in the corner–they are dry now, put them on.

Judah darted to the corner to dress quickly, although Julia continued to watch him eagerly. She seemed to relish, he thought, the last few moments of his shame before her.

Julia continued again:

I support myself with these herbs and remedies. I learned them from an old priestess in my village. But the physicians could not bear the competition from me. Who wants to pay some arrogant Greek filled with books to poke and prod you and babble all sorts of theories that make no sense, when a quick draught from me fixes you right up? And, at half the price. This one young physician, so impressed with himself and all his studies in Athens, he hated me more than any of the others ever did. Tall man with a big wobbling belly, who had this way of looking at a sick person like she was an ant that had tried his patience and needed stepping on. Still, he was a clever one. Riled up the local Christian priest, said I must be a witch consorting with Satan, and when someone important in town died–people always die, nothing you or I can do to stop that– that physician and that priest convinced the authorities to arrest me. So I ran into the forest.

All my old customers still see me, every one. They know Julia is honest and her remedies work. They just need to be, how should I put it? ... Discreet. Yes, discreet–they come here quietly and do not go talking about where I am and what I am doing. Will you promise to keep my secret?

Of course. It is the least I can do to repay your kindness.

Julia stroked his chest gently through his tunic. Her touch made him uneasy, but it still felt warm and good, far better than being alone, wet and shivering, in the dark woods.

So Reuven, why were you traveling through the forest? Where did you want to go? Maybe I can help you find your way.

She kept stroking his chest with one hand and grazed his cheek with her other hand. Judah's breath grew heavy and he trembled. What is happening? he thought. This woman is not my wife, not a Jew, not even pretty–she stinks of some foul plant and has a furry mole between her lip and her nose.

But Judah felt unable to tear himself away. All he wanted was to draw closer to Julia, although he told himself this was folly–he knew he should push her away and leave, but at the same time he did not want to. She kissed him, and then Judah, for the first time, yielded to the full and complete delights of physical love.

VII. To the Mountain of Venus

WHEN JUDAH AWOKE there was a sliver of moonlight trickling into the hut, and by its light he could see he was lying next to Julia. There was a faint gurgling, bubbling sound. He figured at first there must be a stream or a brook nearby, but as the sound grew louder, he realized it was coming from inside the hut. In his confusion, Judah made a sudden turn that jostled Julia, who flipped inertly to her side. A torrent of water gushed out of her mouth, stinking of sea salt.

Judah froze in terror. Two women have drowned now in a bed next to me, he thought. I will never be able to defend myself. No doubt my head will be sliced clean off in some public square. But, it is a lie—I am innocent. He wanted to cry at the smugly satisfied, judgmental faces in the crowd he imagined to be cheering his execution. Their contempt morphed into disgust—how dare you still refuse to acknowledge your guilt, they hissed back. There was no point in speaking to them.

Judah ran away from the hut into the nighttime forest until he came to a stream where, parched from his sprint, he drank greedily and washed his face and hair. Taking a deep breath, he stood back up, and began to walk again, albeit more slowly.

After a few paces, he felt as if he was watched, yet saw no one about. Soon the ground around him became wet, even though there had been no rainfall. The stream was right behind him again, as a newly formed tributary had just cut a meandering path directly to his feet. So Judah swerved away in a new direction, where he saw there was only dry ground. Yet several minutes later the stream's tributary was again nipping at his feet, as if the water were following him.

Judah ran, but every way he went, the water followed right behind, modulating its speed to remain in synch, always keeping just behind his feet. As the sun rose, he took a sharp turn to escape the stream, but suddenly saw that there was a second stream careening towards him.

The two streams soon changed strategy: instead of following him, each one would alter its flow to force Judah to run in a particular direction to evade it. And, they both began to smell of bitter, sharp sea salt.

Exhausted from the hunt, Judah eventually climbed up a large tree, where he collapsed on a thick branch into a black, dreamless sleep. When he woke, the sun was high in the sky—it appeared to be noon, if not slightly later. His limbs ached from leaning against the hard, uneven branch, and his belly was sore from hunger. He breathed deeply in the still forest, trying to clear his addled mind.

Yet Judah felt once more as if he was watched by someone. Meanwhile his left leg had gradually slipped down, without him noticing, until his foot was hanging a few feet below the branch. There was a sudden splash of water on his toes, and then another, and yet another.

Judah looked down and recoiled in terror: the two streams had stopped at the base of the tree right where he had climbed up. Up from them now sprang two geysers that reached almost to Judah's dangling foot. And on top of each geyser was a woman's head, formed from the water, with a grimacing, angry face and snakes for hair—as if the streams had been sculpted into gorgons.

Filled with dread, he marked out a spot on the other side of the tree from the streams, and jumped. But upon hitting the ground he re-injured his ankle, forcing him to limp forward and grasp branches for support, certain the water gorgons would descend upon him at any moment and drown him in saltwater, just as Rivkah and Julia had been drowned.

The streams overtook him easily and encircled his legs. The gorgon heads rose up, one on each side of him, but they no longer looked directly into his eyes. The circle of water moved forward, and Judah, seeing no escape, stayed in its center and walked forward where he was led by the gorgon heads. Every so often an animal passed—a wild boar, a fox—but it quickly scrambled away in fright once one of the aquatic heads looked into its eyes.

The little procession continued until Judah was led to the foot of a mountain covered in cracked red clay and dotted with stunted shrubs, except for the summit, which was clouded in white mist. Suddenly, the circle of water stopped moving. A gigantic eagle swooped down, gripped Judah in its talons, and flew off with him. But the flight was brief: the great eagle deposited Judah on a small landing further up the mountainside, and departed. On three sides were sheer cliff drops. Turning around, he saw a cave, from which he heard faint sounds—fading, thin echoes of laughter and splashing water.

Lying on the ground, he looked up at the endless blue sky, and the white mist circling the mountain peak, feeling pitifully small next to the awesome scale of nature. How had his life come to this horrible pass? Judah was certain he would die soon—he would accidentally roll over the cliff's edge in his sleep, or be eaten by whatever lived in the cave, or maybe just starve to death.

This was not supposed to be his life. He was to marry Rivkah and raise a family. His life was supposed to be *Shabbat* candles, warm soup, and a small daughter falling asleep on his lap on a rainy spring night. This hideous death all alone on the barren mountainside, and the imminent desecration of his corpse by passing vultures, were not what he deserved. How could he be made to suffer so cruelly? Hadn't he merited more kindness from the universe? Sobbing, gently at first but soon enough in violent torrents, he writhed and moaned until sleep overcame him.

VIII. Inside the Mountain of Venus

ECHOES FROM THE mouth of the cave woke Judah that night. It was a song, faint, sung by a woman. Moving carefully towards the cave to hear it better, he was sure he had heard this song before, but he could not remember when. The song was soothing. He moved ever closer to the cave, until he was inside, and could see in the distance, an orange light—a torch perhaps. Were there people here? he wondered. Perhaps I am not doomed after all.

There was a river, running downhill under the mountain, at the bottom of which appeared the source of the light. At the river's edge, Judah came upon a dock of sorts with a small rowboat tied to it. He pulled the rope to bring the boat closer and stepped in. The lovely song was much clearer now. The words were in Greek, although his Greek was too poor to make out their meaning. But, he desperately wanted to hear more of this song.

Judah did not lift the oars but let the current pull him downhill through what felt like an easy sloping waterway. But then, the ceiling of the cavern edged lower until he was forced to lie on his back. The ceiling was soon only a finger's length from his forehead. This was his end, he was sure—he was trapped; and should the cavern narrow any further he would be crushed. He closed his eyes and buried his face in the bottom of the boat, which now seemed to have a will of its own. It picked up speed in its zigzag descent.

Then the boat stopped. There were now women's voices laughing all around him. Judah sat up again and saw he was inside a vast underground chamber, which was brilliantly lit up, as if by a thousand suns, but there was no source for the light— no opening to the sky, no torches, no lamps. The ceiling and walls were so high and wide that Judah could not see them clearly.

The boat was drifting lazily on a winding river that seemed to weave throughout the immense chamber. Inside the coiling river were islands covered in lush vegetation—tall green grasses, bushes exploding with blue, red and purple berries, and huge trees weighted down with an abundance of pink-yellow fruit. There were statues of Venus erected on the various islands, although no other visible signs of human habitation.

The laughter started up again. Although he saw no one, there were ripples in the water, as if the laughter had ducked underwater to hide. He felt a hard tug on the left side of the boat as two smooth arms reached out of the water. A familiar head emerged and looked Judah in the eyes: the siren who had once danced riotously in the storms by the lighthouse, with her long blue hair, her red lips and red coral necklace, and her green fish tail. With a heave she hurled her body into the rowboat, landing on top of Judah and pinning him down. She grabbed his head and kissed him joyously.

You came home to me, at long last, my dear Judah, my beautiful husband. This will finally be our proper wedding day. I have worn your ring for so many lonely days, longed for you, watched you betray me with other women. But now you are here and now you are mine. I knew in the end you would be faithful to your true wife, to your one beloved.

The siren pulled herself up and leaned her head down to look at Judah. Her long blue hair fell in damp messy waves across her cheek and neck and grazed Judah's face and chest. She pawed his chest like a restless cat. Looking at her beautiful albeit aged and deeply lined face, at the glittering blue hair and red lips and pale skin, he felt dizzy with desire.

But then his mind cleared: this was the murderer of Rivkah and Julia, the demon spirit who had hounded him in the forest, who would not let him live the good decent Jewish life he was supposed to lead. What was he doing? How could he kiss this monster?

The siren's smile faded into a worried frown as Judah recoiled from her. She sighed, closed her eyes, and jumped back into the water. Soon he felt something pushing the boat from underneath. The boat flew into the air and crashed on one of the islands in the cavern's winding river. The impact tossed him off the boat and into a stone statue of Venus reclining on a faded seashell. As he sat up, massaging the bruises on his scalp, he saw the siren standing above him—but her fish tail had turned to legs, and she was wearing a long lime green dress that tightly hugged her curving hips.

You need to eat dear, she said. Your hunger is putting you in a foul mood, and that is not good for our special day.

The siren fell to her knees. In her hands she held a huge pink-yellow fruit–something like a peach, but far bigger than any peach Judah had ever seen. With her sharp, blue-painted nails, the siren sliced pieces of the fruit and dropped them into Judah's mouth.

The fruit was marvelously sweet, and as he ate, his fear and anger drifted away. Judah let his head fall into the siren's lap, floating merrily in the dress's soft fabric. She stroked his cheek, and sang to him, a beautiful, subdued song of love lost and regained. He looked up at her and felt at home. Time and memory dwindled to the point he no longer felt there was such a thing as the past–he had always been right where he was, with this woman, on this island, eating the wondrous fruit, and just like that he would always remain.

When Judah had finished all the fruit, the siren led him to the other side of the island, where there was a small hovel made from branches, leaves and flowers. In the middle of the structure was a canopied bed built for languid afternoons of pleasure, with a mattress filled with water. Judah felt as if he were swimming in the sea as he rolled in bed with the siren.

My husband, she said, we have waited too long. You consecrated me as your wife with this ring, but then you left me and betrayed me. But now, you are where you belong. Come drown in my arms.

And so he did.

When Judah woke later, he was alone on the bed. The cavern's light had dimmed to a dull yellow, but he could still see clearly. He walked out of the hovel without any particular purpose. It simply felt good at that moment to move his legs.

As he strolled back towards the statue of Venus on her seashell, Judah beheld a wondrous sight: everywhere there were fairies–tiny winged women with stern faces, no bigger than hummingbirds, with close-cropped hair and efficient miniature housedresses–who were flying around, their bodies lit up like fireflies. When he approached one or two of them, they rudely brushed him away–the fairies apparently had more important matters to attend to and did not appreciate an outsider in their realm.

Feeling a wave of loneliness crash over him, Judah sauntered slowly to the narrow beach, sat down and sighed. But soon laughter, nearby and raucous, woke him from his sad reverie. A whole gaggle of sirens–more than his foggy brain could easily count–leaped out from the water, giggled and pointed at him and whispered playfully, although he caught none of their conversation.

Finally, one of the sirens tossed several pieces of the same sweet fruit at Judah, who once again ate them gluttonously. The fruit lifted his spirits immediately, and, on a whim, he pulled off his clothes and jumped into the water, landing in the middle of the sirens. Giddy and lightheaded, he started to splash them and they splashed him back. The group swam around the cavern's winding river, as the sirens sang of carefree summer afternoons where nothing serious ever happens and the only difficulty is picking the next harmless prank to play upon an always high-spirited and understanding friend.

Four of the sirens reached for Judah–one grabbing each limb–and swam now, very fast, so fast he thought he should be nauseous, but instead he felt only the wild exhilaration of a super-human speed. The sirens became bored with this game after a time and gently dropped Judah on a different island's beach. He tried to stand, but kept falling over from dizziness, prompting the sirens to squeal with delight. He laughed at himself, too.

The sirens' laughter then suddenly stopped, and their faces grew pale and worried. Judah felt himself lifted up from behind, and there she was again: the blue-haired siren, still sporting legs instead of a tail, but this time wearing a short shift dress the color of moonlight. She laid him down on the beach, and sang songs of devoted lovers who braved terrible trials to be together.

Judah smiled at her in his innocence and joy. He wanted only the siren's love, in a never-ending magic day in the great underground cave.

IX. Expulsion from Paradise

EVERY DAY BECAME a harmless, boisterous delight: splashing with the sirens in the water, singing and embracing and kissing his siren wife, and eating the deliriously wonderful fruit that melted away all pain and worry. Even some of the fairies grew friendlier, and described their labors in making the flowers bloom and the fruit trees grow, although Judah would rapidly lose interest and itch again to splash and race in the river.

But, as time imperceptibly glided away, the fruit steadily lost its power to enchant with each successive round of feasting. The blue-haired siren had sharp words for the fairies and their shoddy workmanship with the fruit trees, but they insisted they were doing their best. Alas, the fairies sighed, humans are cursed to grow accustomed to, and bored with, everything they enjoy, even the fruits of paradise.

As the anesthetic effects of the fruit faded, Judah became tormented by his dreams. People he knew and loved–Rivkah, his parents–were crying out to him in pain, but he could not reach them. He longed for these phantoms and often woke sobbing. As his memories of the past came back, Judah's senses sharpened in the present, too. He noticed how terrified everyone in the cavern was of his siren wife, although he did not know why. The other sirens seemed to force their gaiety with him. But worst of all, he saw how fake the sky was: a clean slab of smoothed over grey rock, lit up somehow, with tacked on little balls that illuminated at night as toy stars for an immense nursery. Judah longed again for the real night sky, which he saw so vividly in his dreams.

His growing curiosity about his surroundings led him to quiz the fairies about the plant life and the various islands. The industrious, earnest fairies were quite forthcoming, as they were glad, at last, there was someone who appreciated their hard work and wide erudition. They explained that the blue-haired siren was a mighty goddess who once had worshippers all across the Roman world. But she had fallen on hard times. The Romans had abandoned her flighty, hedonistic cult for austere chaste Christianity, and she had found herself unwelcome in her former cities. Worse than unwelcome: literally homeless, as her temples and shrines were ransacked or turned into churches. At a loss for a dwelling place on land, she left for the sea, and delighted in the playful ways of the sirens. The goddess found she enjoyed teasing sailors and lighthouse keepers on stormy nights.

But she still needed a home, so she swam deep under water, bored a tunnel to this place, and made this enchanted cavern. The various sirens of the oceans and the seas readily agreed to live with her in this new hidden paradise, as the Christian priests were ill-disposed to their songs and urged pious sailors to slice the demon witches through with harpoons.

The fairies were brought in as a final addition to make sure the flowers and fruit trees would grow. Goddesses and sirens were all fond of the grand gesture, but they lacked the solid focus and attention to detail necessary for effective and sustainable horticulture.

Judah duly noted how impressed he was with the fairies' dedication and consummate skill. He asked them how many islands there were and whether they preferred one or the other.

The fairies furrowed their brows and debated amongst themselves the merits of the different islands, diving into the minutiae of their gardening craft and drawing fine distinctions between the hue and glow of different plants. Yet they agreed on one point that intrigued him: there was one island they were barred from visiting. It was surrounded by a mist that gave off a foul, rotting odor. The fairies had seen the sirens swimming there, and entering and exiting the mist, but no fairy was permitted to enter upon pain of death.

Did you ask the goddess why that island is forbidden to you?

She would not answer us.

When can I see the sirens swim there?

At twilight, on some days, a siren will get a mean, hungry look in her eyes. Her teeth narrow and sharpen, and she jumps up and down biting at the air. The other sirens back away from her, very carefully. No one will look her in the eye. She moans like she is in horrible pain, and her lovely singing voice dissolves into discordant screaming. After she has been left completely alone she swims to that island. When she reappears from the mist, the siren is her old playful self, singing happy songs.

Watch them at twilight, as we said, if you want to follow one of the sirens into the foul mist. But it seems an ill place to us. Perhaps you will be fine, you are the goddess's favorite and lover, maybe she will protect you from whatever dark spirits crawl at the edges of this place. Or maybe she will take this as betrayal. No need for you to be too curious, you have been blessed by the goddess. Delight in her favors and empty your mind.

But Judah was now too curious.

So each twilight he watched and waited on the beach, yet there were no angry eyes and frenzied leaps, just winsome, coy teasing and indulgent game-playing in the water. As twilight after twilight passed in this easy manner, he wondered if the fairies had been playing a trick upon him.

One such twilight Judah's eye wandered to an orange-haired siren with a bright purple tale and purple lips. Overcome with desire as he gazed into her inviting, flirting eyes, his cares faded and he was tempted to jump after her into the river—although he knew she would flee rather than risk angering the goddess by being too close to him.

Yet soon he saw two angry eyes returning his stare, angrier than he had previously seen in the enchanted cavern. The orange-haired siren shoved another nearby siren away, flashed teeth that had sharpened into vicious knifepoints, and screeched an anguished, raging cry. The other sirens fell silent and ever so discreetly swam to other shores.

Now alone with the furious raging siren, he watched her jump up and down in the air, moaning all the while. She appeared to Judah to be frustrated at her inability to satisfy some throbbing desire in her body. Her dagger-like teeth bit at the air. Her face, which, like the other sirens, had been silken and coquettish, was now covered in jagged lines. Everything that had once shined forth from her–her eyes, her hair, her lips, her tail–faded into a brooding, menacing dimness. She reminded him of a rabid dog he had once seen run through his native city biting and mauling the other dogs and even tearing at a horse's leg with his teeth before a well-aimed sword thrust to the belly finally stopped him.

Although Judah told himself he too should leave this siren before she tore into his flesh, there was something hypnotic about her raging movements and, instead of fright, he felt an overpowering lust. The desire to be with her grew so strong that he dove into the water and swam towards her.

The siren had meanwhile been ignoring him and his intense stare. When he tried to swim close, she shoved him away. Judah watched her continue to leap in and out of the river. Every twitch of her body made him ache with yearning for her, to have those knifepoint teeth tear into his flesh. His lust led him to long to be bled and beaten and sacrificed to the wild siren.

It was hard for Judah to keep up with her. Sirens, because of their powerful tails, are naturally fast swimmers, and the raging siren was shooting through the water even more rapidly than normal. Yet he found strength he did not know was within him and kept pace across several violent turns. The two swam to a far corner of the cavern.

In this place, the sparkling silver river faded into a brown muddy pond. Judah struggled ever harder to swim in the thick ooze, as his lust would not leave him in peace. Tall weeds reaching up from the bottom of the river tangled his legs, but he angrily tore himself free.

The siren approached a thick wall of grey fog, with Judah still close behind her. A hideous stench flooded his nostrils, making him sick to his stomach, but he still swam on. The siren dove into the mist, with a newfound excitement and a shriek of delight. He lost sight of her, but then saw the ripples in the water made by her tail, which he followed straight into the mist.

The fog surrounded a small island, an arid place full of sharp rocks and congealed clumps of red dirt. Yet the island was far from empty. Everywhere dead bodies–dead human bodies–were strewn about. The bodies did not appear to have decomposed in any way, although the overpowering smell indicated they had been rotting for some time. Many of the corpses were heaped in piles.

Although appearing well-preserved, the bodies were nevertheless not fully intact. Each one appeared to have been bitten into, as bite marks and missing patches of skin and eyes and lips were ubiquitous. It was as if a grand buffet had been laid out for snacking vultures.

The sight and stink of the bodies snapped Judah out of the spell of his lust. He heard a jostling to his left, and spun around quickly to see the orange-haired siren again. She had used her arms to drag her body along the beach towards a pile of corpses. With her teeth, she pulled a scrawny bald man's corpse from a teetering pile of bodies. His arms had been completely chewed off, and he was also missing a foot, an eye, and both ears. The siren tossed him into a narrow clearing between piles of bodies. After thoughtfully surveying what was left of him, she smiled, sank her teeth into his left rib cage, and greedily ate.

Judah was terrified, but could not turn away. There was something familiar about the hairless head atop that mutilated body. He inched closer. It was hard to reconstruct what the head must have looked like before the man's face had been mangled by so many bites, but Judah slowly was able to form a mental picture.

And then true terror struck him: it was Tobias, loyal and devoted servant to the goddess Venus, who had answered her inviting song and dove into the sea to his death.

Judah staggered away to the other side of the island. The stink of the corpses knocked him down to his knees, and he vomited again and again as if his body was trying to eject every last piece of sweet fruit he had eaten in this horrible cavern. When he had finally spent all his energy, he collapsed in a faint.

In his dream, he walked among the mangled corpses. Some of the dead bodies denounced him—beast, murderer, devil-worshipper. Others laughed at him: look at him, so pretty with all his pieces still fitted together, but just you wait, pretty man. They sang sweetly to us, too, they flashed their inviting eyes at us, too. And soon enough they sank their teeth into our hides. There is nothing sacred about your fragile flesh and bone. Your turn will come.

When Judah woke the air was fresh and cool again, and he was lying next to a statue of Venus on a tranquil beach. He had no idea how he had been transported back to this place. A soft hand stroked him, and there was a lullaby. He looked up, and there was the blue-haired goddess.

She looked at him with worried, searching eyes.

What troubles you? Ask and it is yours.

Judah looked down, unable to bear the sight of the monster who had built this evil place.

Please, please, unburden your heart. There is nothing but love for you here. Some fruit to make you feel better?

You are a monster.

The goddess looked back now with stunned eyes.

I saw the bodies. You are a murderer. You are a monster. And Tobias, too, he loved you, more than I ever have or ever could. When everyone else abandoned you, he loved you and you murdered him.

The goddess forced a kind smile. Dear, you just had a bad dream. You are confused. Come, sit with me. Look at how lovely the trees are in this light.

Judah shuddered and backed away.

No. You killed them, Tobias and Rivkah and Julia and all of them.

Judah paused. He and the goddess stared at each other silently.

You are a false god. I have sinned terribly by being here. Free me, and let me go back to my home to repent my sins and to beg forgiveness from the one true Holy One, Blessed be He.

The last phrase was spoken in Hebrew.

You are my husband. You pledged yourself to me.

The goddess's face was twisted in anger, but also betrayed a mounting anxiety. Judah wondered if, in a world filled with only Christians and Jews, she was afraid of being left abandoned and alone. For a moment, he felt pity towards her and scolded himself for being cruel. Is she so terrible? Perhaps she simply needs a companion, someone to love and adore her.

But then he recalled her victims: Tobias, who had truly loved her, and whom she had betrayed to his death, Rivkah, who had done her no harm, and did not deserve to have her life cut short. The injustice of the goddess's whims was too much—he could not be her consort.

And what will happen if I stay here, Judah wondered. Will she grow bored with me and feed me to her sirens one afternoon? Or become jealous again? Or will I grow to think there is nothing amiss with a goddess choosing to slit a throat here or there to amuse herself or to soothe a passing feeling of pique? Will I also turn into a monster?

Judah looked back at her. She was overpowering in her desirability—her gently curving body wrapped snugly in a clinging green gown, her blue hair cascading down. Seized with passion for her, his hand involuntarily reached out. The goddess smiled in triumph.

He was ashamed of himself. Images swirled in his mind, objects and places and people flew madly in a wild dance, but eventually they faded until only one remained: his father's *tallit*, that soft white and blue prayer shawl with the long string fringes, which Judah as a little boy would twist around his fingers while his father swayed and chanted in the synagogue. He could smell his father's warm, sweaty body and feel the bristles of his beard.

Judah opened his eyes and stood up.

I cannot stay here any longer. You know this is not my place. I must go home to my family. Which is the way home?

The goddess pleaded with him: Please stay, please stay a little longer.

He refused.

The world out there is not what you think, sweet husband. Time passes differently in my cavern. How long have you been here, do you think?

A few weeks, perhaps. The soldiers have probably given up their search in the forest.

Silly, dear husband, those soldiers are long dead, as is the country they served. Your world, everyone you knew, they are all dead. You have passed centuries here. You have lived much longer than a man is supposed to live. There is nothing for you out there. You and I are the ruins of an old world. We belong together.

Judah remained unmoved: I must go.

If you go, you cannot return. That is the price to divorce me. This wondrous place and its delights are my dowry, and to divorce me you must return my dowry in full. You will be alone out there, in that alien new world, and when you shiver with cold and loneliness, I will not be there to comfort you.

I must go.

The goddess looked at him with pity and regret.

As you wish. Lay down and close your eyes. When you wake, you will have returned my dowry.

X. The Penitent

A HARD REDDISH-GREEN apple fell on Judah's head. He opened his eyes, but was not sure where he was or how he had arrived there. Pulling himself up with the help of a low-hanging tree branch, he saw he had been lying on the ground in an apple orchard. The sun was shining above–the real sun with its refreshing lively light, not the strange unnatural glow of the goddess's cavern. He felt strong, well-rested and well-fed.

Judah smiled broadly as he realized that he had escaped from the demon monster and her underground lair. This was again the surface of the Earth, hard dirt and warm sunshine. He was determined to return home to his family, clear his name, find a new Jewish woman to marry, and lead the life he had intended to lead.

But first, Judah had to figure out where the goddess had dropped him. The apple trees had been planted in neat rows, with a gravel path winding through them. Following this path in the hopes of finding some sort of steward or caretaker, each step felt invigorating as he filled his lungs with real, outdoor air.

The orchard turned out to be quite large. Judah picked the occasional apple as he happily meandered along. For the first time, he thought, I can truly taste an apple. An apple does not overpower with sweetness or numb one's capacity to remember—no, it satisfies your needs, unobtrusively, not too bitter and not too sweet. The apple is a good, honest fruit, a helper and not a seducer.

The sun had started setting by the time Judah reached the archway separating the orchard from what appeared to be a modest country villa. As there was no one in sight, he sauntered jauntily towards the villa's door and gave a loud knock, which was answered, after a brief pause, by a short round man with a sparse, unkempt beard.

Greetings friend, I am Judah, a merchant from the port city of ----------. I have become lost, and I am trying to figure out the way back. Do you know the way? Is there an inn nearby where I could find a bed and a meal?

The fat man gave a puzzled look, and appeared to have understood nothing. He mumbled a response in a language that Judah did not recognize.

Can you speak Latin? Judah asked.

The man made more mumbling, almost gurgling sounds, in his bizarre dialect. Judah took a different tack and repeated his question in broken Greek. But this worked no better. Running short on languages, he even tried a phrase or two in Hebrew, but to no avail.

The man scratched one of the more thickly grown beard patches on his cheek before turning around and shouting more incomprehensible things in his strange language. Once these words, whatever they were, had whipped the house's residents into a frenzied commotion, the fat man motioned for Judah to follow him inside.

The interior of the villa was modest, with bare wooden walls and poorly made wooden furniture. As there were no murals on the walls, or mosaics on the floor or ceiling, the house struck Judah as surprisingly dreary, as if its owner had perversely decided to banish all the standard issue beauty of a properly decorated home in the Roman Empire's Western provinces.

After leading Judah into a dining room, the man directed him to sit down and then scampered off. Eyeing his surroundings, Judah noticed an immense crucifix hanging on the wall. So at least this is a Christian home, I am likely somewhere in the Roman Empire. But it struck him as odd that his host could speak neither Latin nor Greek.

Soon the fat man returned with a group of people, whom Judah guessed were his wife, children, and servants. They recited a solemn, intense prayer in their strange language and then launched into rapid conversation, at times erupting in rage, but then quickly pivoting to smiles and laughter. It was all a mystery to Judah, but he appreciated this family's kind hospitality to him. Dinner was plentiful—roasted vegetables, bread, cheese, and venison.

Towards the end of the meal, another short round man entered the room. This one appeared to be a few years younger than the master of the villa and was clean-shaven. He was dressed in what appeared to Judah to be an oversized burlap sack with holes cut for his arms and head, although he wore an imposing iron cross around his neck. This new man's head was bald except for a thin circle of messy, disheveled tufts of hair ringing his scalp.

The man in the sack approached the villa's owner and the two pointed at Judah and spoke in their own language some more. After a while, the two fat men motioned for Judah to follow them into a side alcove.

The man in the burlap sack addressed some words to Judah in their language.

Judah replied in Latin: I do not understand your language.

To Judah's relief, the man in the sack replied in Latin: I speak Latin, too. But how is it that you can speak Latin and not the common tongue?

I grew up speaking Latin. Until today, everyone I had ever met spoke some Latin, except the occasional sailor from the East who speaks only Greek. But no one here speaks Greek or Latin. Where is this place?

The man in the sack furrowed his brow. Where are you from, stranger? I know of no place where even the serfs speak Latin. I am Brother Timothy, one of the brothers of the Abbey of -----.

I am Judah, from the port city of -------. And everyone in the Western Empire speaks Latin.

I have never heard of your city. And even though you speak Latin, which leads me to believe that you must have received a proper Christian education from the Church, your name is unusual for a Christian. Come with me, we must consult the abbot.

And so Brother Timothy led Judah out the villa door again, to a waiting wagon, with horses already hitched and the coachman tapping his foot impatiently. Once the passengers had boarded, they rode in silence through a dusty country road in the hazy purple light of the twilight hour. Judah was feeling quite tired by this time and decided to save his questions for the monastery's abbot.

It was past nightfall when the wagon reached the courtyard of the abbey. Brother Timothy led Judah into a small room, where he asked him to wait. Judah was once again struck by the bareness of his surroundings: no mosaics, no murals, nothing but a small crucifix dangling precariously in front of the peeling white paint. The bright moon shining into the cell filled him with hope: Soon, very soon, I will walk under that moon in my city's harbor and watch the ships and feel the breeze from the sea.

Brother Timothy returned. This way, he said, pointing towards a long darkly lit corridor. Sad muffled chants emerged from various rooms as the two men walked through the forbidding hallway. Judah could not understand why the atmosphere was so heavy with mourning, but he reminded himself that he would soon be gone and that he had escaped a far more dangerous enclosure than this.

Brother Timothy led him to a large, brightly illuminated room, in the center of which sat a powerfully built man behind a stone desk piled high with books and letters. The man was dressed like Brother Timothy—the same sack and metal cross around his body, the same spare circle of hairs around a bald scalp—but he also sported a thick grey beard. Judah thought there was something sympathetic and understanding about his eyes—an indulgent, forgiving lord of the manor.

Brother Timothy silently bowed and exited. The man, whom Judah surmised to be the abbot, gestured for him to sit down on a wooden stool. The abbot looked Judah up and down for a minute, scratched his beard and asked softly, in Latin, who Judah was and where he was from.

Judah replied with his name and his city, then thanked the abbot for his gracious hospitality and asked for directions home.

Please, son, repeat the name of your city again?

Judah did so.

I know the city, but it has not gone by that name for hundreds of years. What is the year of our lord now?

It is the year -----, in the reign of Emperor -----.

The abbot leaned forward. Are you certain? About the year and the emperor?

Of course, Judah replied.

The abbot stared at him hard for a few moments, and eventually let out a sigh.

You seem to truly believe what you say. But, my son, it is more than five hundred years later. Where were you baptized? And how can you speak such perfect Latin and be totally ignorant of the common tongue?

Judah began to feel uncomfortable. He had not wanted to believe the goddess's words that centuries had passed, which he had assumed merely to be a trick to keep him captive longer in her evil cavern. Once more he told himself it was impossible for so much time to have passed—no human man could live hundreds of years. Doing his best to remain composed he answered with a forced calmness:

My lord, I was never baptized. I am a Jew. Latin is the common tongue spoken by everyone in my city. I studied Greek and Hebrew at school, although I have never mastered either one. But, you must be playing a trick about the year.

You are a Jew, you say?

Judah nodded.

A Jew who speaks Latin as fluently as the bishop. This is a strange mystery.

The abbot scratched his beard.

It is late, my son, and you have clearly had a long, arduous day. You should lie down and rest. In the morning, we shall see about clarifying these matters.

The abbot called out for Brother Timothy, who promptly reappeared and escorted Judah to a different room. There was no light there except for the moon peeking through the iron bars of a circular window, and once again, the walls were bare save for a crucifix. Brother Timothy showed him to a narrow wooden bed with a torn wool blanket.

The next morning Judah woke to the sound of more anguished, murmuring chants. He yawned, rose, and stepped into the hallway. Two tall, gaunt men saw him and whispered quickly to each other. A moment later, Brother Timothy grasped his arm and brought him to a spacious room where many of the brothers sat on benches eating quietly. Timothy brought food to Judah, a bland, hot cereal of some sort.

After breakfast, Brother Timothy led Judah outside again to the front courtyard, where the two men were soon joined by a third. Brother Timothy introduced Brother Benedict, a young novice at the monastery. As Brother Timothy explained, Brother Benedict had been born a Jew in the nearby town, but had been blessed by God in His great mercy with knowledge of the truth of Christianity and had abandoned the errors and follies of his stubborn, blind ancestors. Nevertheless, Brother Benedict still knew the Jews' dialect, which was slightly different from their neighbors, and could find the nearby town's rabbi for Judah.

Brother Benedict and Judah were soon off together on the road. Brother Benedict was quite young–Judah wondered if any hair had ever grown on his cheeks–but had the intense coal-black eyes of an embittered, aged fanatic. Those eyes bore into Judah with hatred. This angry youth unsettled Judah, who felt it better not to attempt conversation.

The wagon entered the town through a gate with a crumbling stone foundation. A middle-aged man, who appeared to be armed, was vomiting and moaning in the sentry post after what Judah guessed had been an evening spent overindulging. Brother Benedict paid him no mind. The town struck Judah as decrepit: ramshackle houses jammed close together and in need of obvious repair, a hideous stench of animal manure everywhere, no marble forum or imposing government edifices or even any gardens. The wagon went slowly through the narrow streets full of potholes. Brother Benedict's glare had grown, if anything, even more menacing and wrathful.

The wagon eventually made its way into a side street, where it stopped in front of a one-story wooden building with a Star of David etched above the doorway. Brother Benedict told Judah to stay seated while he went inside. Benedict entered the vestibule, where a broad, bearded man accosted him and returned Benedict's glare with his own of equal loathing. The two men spoke tensely and quietly.

Brother Benedict returned to the wagon and told the coachman to proceed to the house with the blue shutters at the end of the street. Once they had arrived, Brother Benedict instructed Judah to follow him. Benedict pushed the door open without announcing his presence and stormed inside. Judah paused at the threshold to kiss the *mezuzah* on the doorpost. Benedict barked at Judah in Latin to get inside.

An old woman in a faded kerchief emerged from the kitchen humming merrily, but she turned pale and trembled when she saw Brother Benedict. He shouted something at her in one of these languages Judah could not understand. The woman disappeared into the rear of the house, then reappeared, and showed the two visitors into a back room.

This room was spacious, but filled with dust particles glittering in the morning sun and the smell of old paper and ink. There were manuscripts and scrolls and letters everywhere, all of them, Judah noticed, in Hebrew script. In the middle of this disorganized pile was a plain wooden desk, and behind the desk was a tiny, serene man with a deeply lined face and a thick grey-white beard. Unlike the other townspeople, this man displayed no fear or hatred of Benedict. Rather, he looked upon Brother Benedict with what struck Judah as pitying eyes.

He and Benedict spoke for a few minutes, although again Judah understood nothing. Brother Benedict then addressed Judah in Latin in a tightly controlled monotone:

Sir, this is Rabbi Kalonymus, son of Meshullam, the esteemed leader of the Jews of this city. As you say you are a Jew, despite being ignorant of their language, you are under his jurisdiction, and not the jurisdiction of our order or the Holy Church. I am here to act as interpreter. The rabbi, like many Jews, knows no Latin. Tell me what words you wish to address to the rabbi.

Judah felt the weight of his troubles float away, as he was finally with his own people again. He addressed the rabbi through his interpreter:

My name is Judah, I am from the Jewish community of the port city of ------. I wish to return home to my mother and my father. Do you know the way?

After these words were translated for him, Rabbi Kalonymus replied he had never heard of such a city.

Judah now became nervous again. He asked the rabbi to confirm that it was the year such and so, using the Jewish calendar.

The rabbi gently replied that the current year was more than five hundred years later than Judah thought. He asked why Judah could not speak the language of the Jews if he was a Jew, but could only speak the language of the Christian priests.

Judah replied that, where he was from, everyone, Jew and Christian, spoke Latin.

The rabbi asked Judah and Brother Benedict to wait out front, in the kitchen, while he consulted the wise words of the holy sages, may their memory be for a blessing, upon this strange matter.

The shy old woman served small pieces of honey cake and cups of mead to her guests while they waited upon the rabbi's deliberations. Judah smiled at her in gratitude, mumbled a blessing in Hebrew (although he was not sure he had the right one), and ate and drank with gusto. This was much better than the monastery's gruel. Brother Benedict ate nothing, but closed his eyes tightly and muttered various Christian prayers.

Rabbi Kalonymus eventually summoned the visitors back into his study. This time he motioned for Judah to sit on a stool next to him. The rabbi bent down, grabbed Judah by the temples, and pushed the tip of his nose almost against the tip of Judah's nose as he stared intensely into Judah's eyes and re-cited various Hebrew incantations.

When he was finished, the rabbi staggered back, his face filled with horror, and his body trembling. Brother Benedict translated his words:

Your soul is putrid and rotted, you have fornicated with demon women and abandoned the Holy One, Blessed be He. You are a hideous stain upon the holy community of Israel.

For the first time, Judah fully grasped how much he had lost and how alone he had become. Groping for an answer, he at last blurted out:

But, great rabbi, revered teacher, I was bewitched and con-fused. I broke free of their clutches, I want to rejoin the Jewish people, and I seek to repent. What is my penance? Say it and it will be done.

Rabbi Kalonymus sighed and absent-mindedly twisted his wedding ring around his finger. His eyes avoided Judah's face.

Please, rabbi, let me repent. The gates of repentance are never closed. Somewhere in these scrolls, in this room, a wise and holy sage must have surmounted this same problem. Please, I have suffered so much. I only want to return home to my parents, my synagogue, to find a wife.

Rabbi Kalonymus broke out into sad, light laughter.

You don't understand, do you, Reb Judah? Everyone you ever knew is long dead, and their graves desecrated and de-stroyed by who knows what armies in battles so long ago that no one bothers to remember any longer. You have no one left to whom you can repent. Perhaps the Holy One, Blessed be He, in his Infinite and Unknowable Goodness and Perfection, shall find a way to forgive your soul and to repair it. But, there is nothing I can prescribe. I look into your eyes, and through your eyes into your soul, and I see nothing Jewish. I see blind maggots crawling and jostling, and I smell rot and decay. With an effort, I can see your sins and I can see the slithering she-demons who reduced you to this state. Souls like yours suffer justly in *gehenna* for eternity.

Have you ever thought about *gehenna*? It is an everlasting prison for the wicked. That can only be so if some souls are so defiled that there is no more opportunity for repentance, such that they could merit an eternal sentence of damnation. You should have died long ago and been judged by the Heavenly Tribunal before the Throne of Glory in the World to Come. Yet you are here. So who knows, perhaps there is a reason? You are a ghost from long ago. You do not belong here. So, go, wander the earth, tell ghost stories to the living, and do not spend the day where you have spent the night. Perhaps the mystery will unravel on your journey. Perhaps, if you suffer enough, the Holy One will accept your penance.

Rabbi Kalonymus yawned and rubbed his eyes and retired to take a nap.

Judah felt numb. Nothing made sense: the immense passage of time without him realizing it, the curse of his fate, the exhortation to solitary wandering. It all felt unreal, as if he were trapped in an unusually vivid dream from which he truly wanted to wake, but could not.

Brother Benedict picked him up by the shoulder and shoved Judah's limp, obedient frame out of the house and into the wagon again. Before Judah realized what had happened, he found himself in the cart leaving the Jewish Quarter and its contentedly snoring rabbi.

Benedict spit out the side of the wagon every time he saw a Jew in the streets. He turned to Judah with a wan smile:

I studied for years with that old man, when I was a boy and then into early manhood. He spun his cobwebs of lies in my mind and obscured the light of God's truth. But then, one day I was given a sign. I had been feeling exhausted–my father's haggling with the matchmakers had been too drawn out, the rabbi's lessons had grown ever more esoteric and difficult– all the troubles of a fine young Torah scholar.

So, to have some respite from my sufferings, I went walking one night into the forest, deeper and deeper. I felt tired but could not stop–some force pulled me. I became lost but kept going. And then the rain pounded down, and I needed shelter, so I turned around and saw an abandoned chapel, next to the ruins of a lord's hunting lodge. I entered the chapel to escape the rain. I shivered from the lashing, biting winds that swooped in through the open windows, and I collapsed onto the stone floor. When I looked up, I could see in the dim light that I was at the feet of a statue of the Holy Virgin Mother. She turned her head to me and bent down and cried. Her tears fell on me, they warmed me, and I felt her boundless love. It was then that I knew I had been reared in the den of falsehood, and I would only find peace and genuine wisdom in the bosom of the Church. Soon after, I ran away from the filthy Jewish Quarter and the Abbott baptized me into the true faith.

I tell you this story because of the rabbi's horrible words to you today. He sees nothing but law and judgment, and you are a condemned man in his unloving, unmerciful eyes. But you can achieve salvation if you open your heart to the truth and to the great love that is in the Church.

Judah did not respond. He could not believe that the God of Israel had abandoned him. There must be a way to mend my ripped soul, he told himself. Something. Perhaps the rabbi is right, and I must wander ceaselessly to learn the secret wish of the Holy One, Blessed be He, for my fate. Or maybe that wandering is my penance, but he did not want to say it outright. Yes, I will wander and beg and atone for my sins. I will let the flesh on my bones wither away from hunger and cold, and that dwindling flesh will be my sacrificial offering to the Holy One, Blessed be He.

And thus Judah, convinced himself of his future salvation.

XI. The Wandering Jew

THE VILLAGERS AND farmers would gossip about him and gawk at him: the wandering mad priest. Not that this priest performed sacraments, preached sermons, or engaged in any other clerical duties. No, the man was assumed to be a priest because he would only speak in Latin, and only a priest could know Latin so well–thus reasoned the sunburnt, exhausted toilers in the countryside.

The mad part was easier for them. The man was a smelly, wrinkled mess in his torn rags. Nor would this man spend the day where he had spent the night, but always insisted on moving on to the next town to beg. But even more telling of his madness, according to this general consensus, was the fact that he insisted he was a Jew even though his refusal to speak any tongue but Latin clearly proved he was a priest.

The same thing happened with each arrival in a new town or village. The madman would come in from the road ranting and begging, but no one could understand a word he said. So someone would fetch the local priest, who would speak kindly, at first, to the stranger, as both men could converse in Latin.

But, invariably, this conversation became heated when the madman insisted over and over that he was a Jew and belonged with the Jews in their quarter.

Sometimes the priest would throw his hands up in despair and sigh sadly at this deluded, clearly fallen Christian brother—for no Jew knew Latin this well, no one who was not educated in the Church could know Latin so well. Shaking his head, the priest would order bread and water for the madman. Occasionally there was an attempt to give him communion, but he always angrily refused, clinging fiercely to his claimed Jewishness.

Yet other priests eventually believed him—after all, why would he insist so passionately that he was a member of the despised, defeated Jewish nation unless it were true? So, they would turn him over to the leaders of the closest Jewish community. But the real Jews could not converse with this madman, because they knew no Latin and he did not speak either Hebrew or any of their dialects. These meetings rapidly degenerated into a squabble between the priest and the Jews as to who bore responsibility for the beggar's food and shelter, each insisting that the madman was the other's responsibility.

Such was Judah's fate in this hostile, diminished world. Initially fired up by the words of Rabbi Kalonymus, he had eagerly embraced the fate of a wandering beggar, sure that his sins would be cleansed and then there would be a sign of his salvation. Every insult and kick felt like a milestone on the road to repentance for his sins with the goddess and her flesh-eating sirens.

Yet as the days and weeks melted into months and years, nothing happened. Judah withered away, sickly and frail, but he could neither experience the release of death, no matter how hideously his bones rattled, nor was there any sign of forgiveness from the Holy One. The days and the faces and the villages ran together in his mind, as a hopeless melancholy crept through his soul.

Memories of the past bubbled up to comfort him. He willed himself to embrace what he was sure were the proper memories to long for: his wife, his parents, his boyhood synagogue, his old daydreams of being an indulgent, balding, pot-bellied Jewish father. But these thoughts brought him no joy, and instead only heightened the sharpness of his pains.

Until one afternoon, exhausted and sore from walking in the scorching heat, Judah shuffled away from the side of the road and collapsed into a deep sleep under the shade of a gnarled old tree. When he woke, at twilight, he saw a pond not too far off in which a huge water lily was floating. The flower appeared to Judah's imagination to be a luxurious sofa, fit for a decadent and imperious queen of the sea. In his mind he saw her again: with blue hair and red lips and a crown of coral, jumping out of the water with the scales of her green fishtail glistening and then lying sideways on the lovely water lily where she beckoned her husband, her lover, to come join her. Ever so faintly, her song wafted about him in the sunset.

Without realizing it, Judah had waded into the pond, his feet giving way in the mud, and only a low-hanging branch hitting his nose roused him back to his senses. After using the branch to rescue himself from the danger of slipping under the water, he sat down on a patch of grass near the pond, closed his eyes, and let himself be flooded with memories of his majestic goddess and her enchanted cavern.

He soon lived within these sinful memories, and thought of nothing but her sweet kisses and her melancholy songs and her delicious fruit. How could I have spurned her wondrous love, he lamented. She gave me bliss, she blessed me with a magical abundance, and I treated her cruelly in return. I failed in my faith in her. She would never have betrayed me the way she betrayed Tobias. I was her true beloved, I was different from other men to her, yet I was too inconstant and fearful to accept her blessing. The way her eyes gazed at me, with such love, and the tenderness with which she sang to me …

So now Judah prayed fervently to the goddess, whose other devotees had perished centuries ago. In a groveling tone, he begged to be reunited with his bride and repented dearly for his ingratitude and lack of faith. Yet the goddess did not respond.

He tried to find her mountain with her enchanted cavern. Following the directions of the village priests, he eventually made his way into the closest mountain range. But there were no desolate crags covered in red clay and thistles. Everywhere, the mountains were lush with trees and grass and churches and monasteries, as if the Christians had exiled her once again from her temple and dwelling place. There seemed to be no trace of her left.

It was an afternoon in late autumn on one of these mountains. The falling leaves were a riot of sad, dark colors—reds and browns and faded oranges, strewn so thickly upon the road that Judah could not see where he was walking anymore. The wind smacked his skin harshly, and he shivered miserably. There was a drizzle of rain on his head that soon grew into a violent torrent.

He staggered forward as best he could, searching for a possible shelter, until he spied a crumbling old stone building in the distance that still had some of its roof intact. Judah huddled in the corner that offered the most protection from the storm, and waited out the downpour. The building was overgrown with vines on its walls and weeds breaking through the weather-beaten floor, but its structure was still somewhat intact—the walls still stood, and most of the ceiling remained. The floor tiles were broken and faded, but there had clearly once been a mosaic depicting a blue sea and a giant seashell carrying a lovely maiden.

When the cold sun returned, Judah explored the ruin. As best he could discern he was in an anteroom with broken benches. Through an interior archway, he came upon a narrower room where the ceiling was fully intact and a thin light penetrated through the occasional narrow hole in the wall. In the semi-darkness, there was something discernible in the back of this room—a statue of someone.

He approached closer. As his eyes grew accustomed to the dark, he recognized the idol—it was her, his goddess, abandoned in this ruin. Her face and hair were intact, as were the folds of her dress, but arms were missing and so was a foot. Her crown was chipped in places, and there were ruins of an altar to the left of the statue.

Judah fell to his knees and embraced the dirt-speckled, icy marble dress and kissed it. Shaking uncontrollably, he grabbed her desperately and sobbed piteously and loudly in the ruin in the forest.

The last loyal acolyte of the once regnant goddess moaned for the gift of her song and sweet kiss, but there was no answer anymore from the old gods.

Other Books by Barak Bassman

Elegy of the Minotaur

Repentance: A Tale of Demons in Old Jewish Poland

King Solomon and Ashmedai: A Wisdom Tale

www.ingramcontent.com/pod-product-compliance
Lightning Source LLC
Chambersburg PA
CBHW032020180726

48283CB00008B/2760